"Well, Sheriff Reno, I think you'll find that the word nice *doesn't exactly apply to me," Ashlyn admitted.*

He looked at her, his eyes boring into her soul.

Ashlyn allowed her own gaze to skim over the sheriff's hard body. Maybe being arrested by this lawman wouldn't be such a horrible thing.

She grinned, her heart beating a little faster. Wouldn't her rich father kill her if she got involved with blue-collar Sam Reno, foster brother of the man who'd nearly ruined her family?

Then again, Sam Reno had his own powerful reasons for hating her kin.

And he probably *would* arrest her if he could read her thoughts....

Dear Reader,

Spring is a time for new beginnings. And as you step out to enjoy the spring sunshine, I'd like to introduce a new author to Silhouette Special Edition. Her name is Judy Duarte, and her novel *Cowboy Courage* tells the heartwarming story of a runaway heiress who finds shelter in the strong arms of a handsome—yet guarded—cowboy. Don't miss this brilliant debut!

Next, we have the new installment in Susan Mallery's DESERT ROGUES miniseries. In *The Sheik & the Virgin Princess,* a beautiful princess goes in search of her long-lost royal father, and on her quest falls in love with her heart-meltingly gorgeous bodyguard! And love proves to be the irresistible icing in this adorable tale by Patricia Coughlin, *The Cupcake Queen.* Here, a lovable heroine turns her hero's life into a virtual beehive. But Cupid's arrow does get the final—er—sting!

I'm delighted to bring you Crystal Green's *His Arch Enemy's Daughter,* the next story in her poignant miniseries KANE'S CROSSING. When a rugged sheriff falls for the wrong woman, he has to choose between revenge and love. Add to the month Pat Warren's exciting new two-in-one, *My Very Own Millionaire*—two fabulous romances in one novel about confirmed bachelors who finally find the women of their dreams! Lastly, there is no shortage of gripping emotion (or tears!) in Lois Faye Dyer's *Cattleman's Bride-To-Be,* where long-lost lovers must reunite to save the life of a little girl. As they fight the medical odds, this hero and heroine find that passion—and soul-searing love—never die....

I'm so happy to present these first fruits of spring. I hope you enjoy this month's lineup and come back for next month's moving stories about life, love and family!

Best,

Karen Taylor Richman
Senior Editor

Please address questions and book requests to:
Silhouette Reader Service
U.S.: 3010 Walden Ave., P.O. Box 1325, Buffalo, NY 14269
Canadian: P.O. Box 609, Fort Erie, Ont. L2A 5X3

His Arch Enemy's Daughter

CRYSTAL GREEN

Silhouette

SPECIAL EDITION™

Published by Silhouette Books

America's Publisher of Contemporary Romance

To Tonya: You were one of Earth's brightest angels.
We miss you.

 SILHOUETTE BOOKS

ISBN 0-373-24455-X

HIS ARCH ENEMY'S DAUGHTER

Copyright © 2002 by Chris Marie Green

This edition published by arrangement with Harlequin Books S.A.

Visit Silhouette at www.eHarlequin.com

Printed in U.S.A.

Books by Crystal Green

Silhouette Special Edition

Beloved Bachelor Dad #1374
*The Pregnant Bride #1440
*His Arch Enemy's Daughter #1455

*Kane's Crossing

CRYSTAL GREEN

lives in San Diego, California, where she has survived three years as an eighth-grade teacher of Humanities. She's especially proud of her college-bound AVID (Advancement Via Individual Determination) students who have inspired her to persevere.

When Crystal isn't writing romances, she enjoys reading, creating poetry, overanalyzing movies, risking her life during police ride-alongs, petting her parents' Maltese dogs and fantasizing about being a really good cook.

During school breaks, Crystal spends her time becoming readdicted to her favorite soap operas and traveling to places far and wide. Her favorite souvenirs include travel journals—the pages reflecting everything from taking tea in London's Leicester Square to backpacking up endless mountain roads leading to the castles of Sintra, Portugal.

THE KANE'S CROSSING GAZETTE

Spencer Socialite Meets Her Match?
by Verna Loquacious, Town Observer

Greetings from your friendly neighborhood grapevine!

Though our cozy hamlet has suffered from a dry spell as of late, I believe I've come upon a veritable sea of gossip.

Ashlyn Spencer, great-great-great-granddaughter of our beloved town founder, Kane Spencer, has been seen on the arm of the new sheriff, Sam Reno. Now, I have to tell you, I'm a tad stunned by this news. For those of you who haven't been keeping up with current—or even ancient—events, Sheriff Reno grew up in these parts, and has recently returned to reunite with his foster brother, Nick Cassidy.

There's been a flood of bad blood between those rich-as-Croesus Spencers and the blue-collar Renos, especially after the factory accident— the one that killed poor Sam's father, bless his soul.

Land sakes, you'd think our socialite Spencer wouldn't dare disappoint Daddy by dating the low-born Sheriff Reno. But, like you, folks, I do love a good star-crossed tale....

Chapter One

Ashlyn Spencer was in a real fix this time.

"Emma, why don't you put away that shotgun?" she asked while backing out of the insect-buzzed porch light and into the shadows. She felt erased, almost safe in the darkness cast by Mrs. Trainor's roof.

The older woman's outline didn't budge from the screened door. "I'll be darned if you play any April Fool's jokes on Trainor property, Miss Spencer. You, me and my sawed-off friend will wait right here until the sheriff comes."

Ashlyn wanted to speak up in her defense, to tell Emma that she wasn't playing any pranks tonight— hadn't played any for a long time now. In fact, this bundle of crisp one-hundred-dollar bills she held in her hand was sticking to her palm with the urgency of a cat clinging to a curtain for safety.

Right about now, they were all victims of worst-case-scenario shotgun nightmares.

"Emma, I—"

A deep voice rumbled over her protestations. "Lower your gun, Emma."

Ashlyn could hear the woman's sigh of relief, even through a screen mashed with Kentucky flies and a trace of dandelion down.

The sheriff and his boots thumped their way up the stairs, onto the porch. "You put that firearm away, Emma?"

A heavy clicking sound from behind the older woman's door made Ashlyn start from her hiding place. Was Emma Trainor cocking the gun?

Ashlyn jolted backward and smashed right into the new sheriff, his chest as broad and as hard as a wall. Not literally, but it felt like so many hard bricks piled together—enough to make her see stars.

She turned to him, blinking, the towering shadow of the sheriff's body eclipsing the moonlight with a heavy jacket. The stars blurring her sight settled into one dull glint on his broad chest. A lifeless, silvery badge.

Fleeting images of Sheriff Carson, the old law of Kane's Crossing, flashed through her mind. He'd liked to give her a hard time for the way she'd run around town, getting into her share of mischief. And her father had paid the sheriff well to keep his daughter in line.

But Sheriff Carson had passed away a short time ago, and a new lawman had taken his place just last month. A man who'd been appointed by the prominent citizens of Kane's Crossing.

Sam Reno had returned to town. The same man

who'd been the object of Ashlyn's star-in-the-eyes fantasies, her Teen Beat dreams.

She gulped and subtly tried to stand behind him, just in case Emma was aiming in her direction.

The other woman stepped onto the porch, and Ashlyn felt her face heat up when she realized that the "click" had merely been the screened door opening.

Emma nodded to the sheriff. "Thanks for answering so fast. I heard an intruder out here and found Ashlyn Spencer lurking around my door."

Ashlyn hid her hands behind her back, hoping no one had seen the money, hoping no one would suspect that she was up to *good* for a change.

Sheriff Reno placed his hands on his lean hips, his silhouette dark against the moon's silver light. "You're going to get someone killed with your weaponry, Emma. Now, I know better than anyone that you want your protection, but pumping bullets into the town socialite won't rid the world of evil. I'd hate to take you in for that."

Ashlyn felt the sheriff shoot her a glance, but she bit her tongue, determined to let them think what they would about her reasons for being here.

Emma stuck her fists into the pockets of her oversize jeans. "Sorry, Sam. I didn't even have a gun. Had to use a fire poker. The girl scared me, sneaking around like she was, creaking my porch boards."

Truth be told, Ashlyn wished she hadn't frightened Mrs. Trainor. The woman had suffered enough pain in her life, what, with her husband dying in the same factory accident that had killed Sam Reno's own father. And she felt partly responsible, too, because it was her family's factory. Her family's responsibility—one that they'd never owned up to.

Sheriff Reno took a step forward into the faint porch light, affording Ashlyn a better vantage point.

He had the corded strength of a Remington sculpture, all rough edges and darkness. His clipped brown hair barely brushed his jacket collar, and it was longer on top, falling to just above his stern brow. The fullness of his lower lip gave her heart a lurch, and it wasn't because he was frowning.

He shook his head, his voice as low and as dry as an endless stretch of desert road. "Well, I guess you can't do a whole lot of damage with a phantom arsenal."

A few more steps brought him closer to Emma. Softly, he asked, "How're you doing?"

The older woman's lips trembled, and Ashlyn had to avert her glance.

"As well as can be expected. Janey's still in the hospital, for as long as the money'll keep her there."

Ashlyn tightened her grip on the hundred-dollar bills and looked up.

Sam Reno cupped his long fingers under the woman's jaw, making Ashlyn's throat ache. His touch was so gentle, so sympathetic, like a physical connection between two survivors who'd lost everything.

She felt invisible, surrounded by the darkness of cave walls, blocking her from the rest of humanity. Dank, lonely, so dark...

Ashlyn washed her mind of those thoughts. She needed to forget about the cave, about the scared seven-year-old girl who'd lived under the banner of town disapproval for so long.

But how could she forget that her family had caused such pain?

Unthinkingly, she cleared her throat, wanting to slap herself when it broke the moment between Emma and the sheriff. He turned to her, a glower of displeasure clearly marking his face.

"What the hell were you doing creeping around here in the dead of night?" he asked.

She tried to shine her most innocent smile, but it didn't quite hold. "I'll have to plead the Fifth on that."

His gaze had focused on her hands, folded behind her back very suspiciously. "Drop it."

That voice—so low, so cold, so deadly serious.

Maybe he thought she was packing her own heat. Heck, if one-hundred-dollar bills were bullets, she'd be absolutely riddled with holes.

She'd give anything for nobody to know what she'd intended to do with the money. Nobody had the right to know.

However, the sheriff's fingers had tensed near his holster, the one with the gun in it.

Ashlyn dropped the wad of money and held her hands in the air, shrugging as she did so. "Whoops."

"Yeah, whoops."

He stepped near her, brushing her sweater with his jacket. As he retrieved the bundle of bills, she shivered, probably because the April night had a sudden warm thrill to it.

He moved in front of her and held up the money. "This should be an interesting explanation."

Emma Trainor's jaw almost hit the floorboards. Why was she so shocked? Was it so unthinkable that

Ashlyn would want to help someone in their time of need?

Well, now she'd have to explain. Unless, of course, she desired an all-expense-paid trip to the sheriff's office.

Actually, she thought, if Sheriff Sam was doing the driving, it didn't sound all that bad.

Ashlyn sighed, donning her "bad girl" facade, planting a hand on her hip, quirking her mouth into a carefree grin. The town expected her to be contrary, running around causing her share of tongue clucking, so why not oblige them?

Her stance hardly reflected the hurt inside. Hurt caused by years of hiding in shadows.

"It'd probably be easier for all of us if I accepted blame and said that this is pocket money. That I was just about to vandalize the Trainor property with some April Fool's flair."

She'd rather die than let them know her real motive. Ashlyn hadn't known Emma's daughter, Janey, very well, but when she'd heard that the insurance company wasn't covering all of Janey's hospital bills, she'd gotten angry. Outraged, as a matter of fact.

She'd figured that it'd be the proper thing to do, leaving some anonymous cash so Janey could pay for her treatments. Breast cancer was costly in more than one way.

But now, from the looks of Emma and Sheriff Reno, Ashlyn knew she had a lot more explaining to do. Fat chance. They'd never believe that a dilettante like her cared about anything. No one in town had ever believed it.

When she focused back on Emma and the sheriff,

they were looking at her as if she'd sprouted a tarnished halo—and it was pierced through her nose, to boot.

Couldn't she have thought of a more creative excuse?

The sheriff hovered over Ashlyn, making her feel about two feet tall. He stuffed the money back into her hand. "Was it too common for you to simply ring Emma's doorbell, maybe send a check through the mail?"

She wanted to blurt out that he was missing the point. She didn't *want* anyone to know that she'd done a kind deed. Ashlyn Spencer was from a greedy family, and half of Kane's Crossing wouldn't pay credence to the rumor of her benevolence anyway. So why try to elaborate?

Sheriff Reno ran his gaze from her head to her curling toes, his expression lingering somewhere between a half-hearted sigh of mirth and a frown of suspicion. She got the distinct feeling that he wasn't used to smiling.

"Let's go," he said, as if she had stolen the money from Emma Trainor and was a certified criminal.

Emma's eyes had softened, her hand reaching out helplessly to Ashlyn. She opened her mouth to say something, then shut it with a smack.

Ashlyn felt like telling her to not apologize after all these years. It was natural to assume that she was up to no good. After all, she'd been making trouble a habit ever since her seventh year, ever since she'd stared at those cave walls and learned a hard lesson or two about life.

As she and Sam turned around to leave, Ashlyn

bent and casually placed the bundle of money on the porch, not even pausing to mark Emma's final reaction. Sam waited for her, then matched her pace as they walked away. When they were out of hearing distance, she couldn't curb a self-protective shrug. "I suppose the fairies told me to do it, Sheriff." She followed up with a sugar-sweet grin.

"Fairies," muttered Sam Reno, shaking his head while he gestured toward his car.

Behind them, Emma's porch light winked off, leaving a sense of moon-bathed quiet. "What, don't you believe in that stuff?" she asked.

They'd moved down the lawn, toward Sam's car. He must have cut his engine at some point, rolling the vehicle to a stop so he could sneak up on Emma and her trespasser with the utmost stealth.

You had to admire that kind of sneakiness, she thought. She would've done the same thing.

He hadn't answered her flippant question, but this silence was killing her need to lighten the mood. So she continued.

"Understand, Sheriff? I'm talking about fairies, sprites, gremlins... You know gremlins are the worst. Downright mean suckers."

More pressing subjects were obviously on his mind. "Trespassing isn't looked on too kindly around here."

That put Ashlyn in her place. "Okay, okay. So at the age of twenty-four, I should be doing more productive things, like sitting around in my baby dolls, popping chocolates and filing my nails. Yeah, that sounds more acceptable, more bourgeoisie. More Spencer-like."

Night creatures serenaded them as they walked.

She became very aware of her choppy breath, the feel of his large body tracking hers.

"What you did for Janey was real nice," he said.

A sarcastic comeback tipped the edge of her tongue. *Yeah, Emma fell all over herself thanking me for the trouble.*

But she kept her peace, not wanting the sheriff to know how much the other woman's judgmental first impression had hurt. Her unwillingness to imagine that Ashlyn could do anything decent was a slap in the face, leaving a mark as dark as her family's reputation.

"Well, Sheriff Reno, I think you'll find that the word 'nice' doesn't exactly apply to me. Besides, I never admitted to doing anything back there."

He stopped and looked at her, his eyes boring into her soul.

Was he a real cop? Sheriff Carson would've taken great umbrage at her blunt tone and shone the flashlight in her eyes in a misguided power trip. He would've hauled her into the jailhouse just for the fun of it.

She allowed her gaze to skim over Sheriff Reno's hard body. Let's see, he'd been two years ahead of Chad, her esteemed brother, in high school...maybe he was around thirty-three.

In her younger years she'd enjoyed making Sheriff Carson chase her around a little, just to get his goat. But this sheriff was in shape, would catch her in a minute flat. Not that being caught by him would be a horrible thing.

She grinned, her heart beating a little faster. He wasn't bad for a thirty-three-year-old. As far as she could see, he had long legs, a flat stomach, arms and shoulders that filled his jacket to great effect...

Wouldn't her father kill her if she got involved with Sam Reno, the foster brother of Nick Cassidy, the man who'd ruined her family?

The whole town had gotten into quite a snit when Nick had strutted right into Kane's Crossing to give her once-wealthy father and brother, Chad, a taste of their own medicine. While both men had been in Europe, Nick had taken over the Spencers' businesses, given them to the poor families in town, teaching her own family a lesson about compassion. Not that the Spencers had learned anything from the debacle. Even now, starch-collared lawyers were scrambling to get back their old properties, to place them back on their self-imposed throne.

And they'd been partly successful, too. The Spencers now had control of their toy factory again, a business they'd sneaked in and purchased with the cunning common to a snake.

She didn't like to be thought of as a snake. Being a normal citizen in Kane's Crossing would've suited Ashlyn just fine.

Sam Reno himself would probably end up with a girl from a normal family—one who reminded him of home-cooked dinners, hand-knit sweaters and white-lace kitchen aprons.

She had to admit though—he was tempting. Her stomach tingled just thinking about snuggling into his jacket, next to his chest, his arms enveloping her with strength.

Then again, Sam had his reasons for hating the Spencers. And he'd probably arrest her out of pure disdain if he could read her thoughts.

She tried to ignore the way his gaze combed over her, the way it slammed her heart against her ribcage. She started walking toward his car, sorry that she hadn't taken her own vehicle out for a cruise tonight.

His voice surged from behind her. "Are you still in college?"

Ashlyn grinned at the small talk, tossing her words carelessly over her shoulder. "Been there, done that, got the T-shirt. Say, you're just giving me a ride home, right? No arrests for trespassing or anything?"

She heard him shifting around his utility belt, adjusting his squawking walkie-talkie. For a minute she thought maybe he was going to cuff her.

"Please, Sheriff. I've got all the silver jewelry I'll ever need."

His long steps caught him up with her, and he stuck out his hand, car keys jangling. "We're just going to my office."

"You *are* arresting me?"

At this point, her golden-boy brother would've whipped out his business card, would've asked the new sheriff if he realized whom he was dealing with. But Ashlyn had never been held in the same esteem as her worshipped brother. Not by the town, thank goodness. And not by her parents.

Did Sam Reno want to make himself look good in front of an upstanding citizen like Emma Trainor? Well, he sure was doing a fine job of carrying out his sheriffly duties.

Sam Reno chuckled, even though she wasn't sure what was so funny.

She said, "You've been living for this moment

your whole life, haven't you, Sheriff? You've just been chomping at the bit to arrest a Spencer.''

Darkness traveled his face, drawing down the edges of his lips, eclipsing the moonlight.

Ashlyn knew she'd opened her mouth one too many times.

Spencer.

The name ripped through his body with razor-blade agony. Seven years ago Sam's father had died in the Spenco Toy Factory under mysterious circumstances. That death had killed his mother, too, from stress and heartbreak. And it'd changed Sam's life. For the worse.

He watched Ashlyn Spencer, assessing the daughter of his worst enemy. She was surrounded by a bleak sky of looming clouds, a drab field of grass. The palette of his life. Even the road running past Emma Trainor's home was empty and desolate.

But Ashlyn herself was a splash of colors—from her bright red sweater to the green and purple string of party beads dancing around her wrist.

Sam tried to feel unaffected as a cloud passed over the moon, almost as if the darkness wanted to hold on to her light for a minute more. She crossed her arms over her chest, her jaunty sweater bellying her obvious agitation.

He decided that the best course of action would be to ignore her comment about arresting a Spencer. "Why're you still in Kane's Crossing, Miss Spencer?"

"Why did *you* come *back* to Kane's Crossing?" she asked, dodging his question.

He knew they were at a verbal stalemate, so he

decided to get this business over and done with. After a moment of heavy silence, he reached out a hand to her. "Let's go."

"To the sheriff's office?"

"It's a hell of a lot warmer than keeping the ghosts company." He allowed his hand to remain, hovering in the air, more of a command than a request.

Maybe he shouldn't even be hauling her in like this, but he'd heard about Ashlyn's propensity for trouble. Better to let her know that the new sheriff meant business. Better to put the fear of the law into her now than later. He could explain himself at the station, where he had the persuasive image of jail cells to back up his warning lecture.

Ashlyn scanned his body again. The first time she'd done it, Sam had merely chalked up the action to curiosity. This time his pulse pounded, awakening feelings he'd packed away over a year ago. Feelings his dead wife had numbed.

He gave Ashlyn Spencer a moment to hesitate, not wanting to make this more serious than it was. She'd been giving money to Emma Trainor, by God. Not only was it an act of someone with a soft heart, but this call was a joke next to the blood and chaos he'd seen as a cop in Washington, D.C.

Wiping away his memories, Sam concentrated on his current problem. Ashlyn took a step forward, the moonlight covering her pixie-featured face with a veil of silver, producing a glimmer in her eye, in her slight smile.

Her forced gaiety made him feel sorry for her, this young woman who'd been called on the carpet for trying to help Emma's family. But the Trainors, like many other people in Kane's Crossing, had been hurt by Ashlyn's kin. Had been stung by their greed time and again.

Her reputation didn't stop him from thinking that Emma had treated Ashlyn unfairly. Had judged her for the company she kept, rather than her actions.

Hell, he could use some of his own advice. Nobody could accuse him of liking the Spencers, especially since they'd been responsible for his father's death.

Sam watched her again as they resumed walking. She'd cut her hair, from what he remembered, which wasn't much. It'd gone from a long waterfall in her younger years to a sandy, short cut, tufts sticking out from her head as if she was a woodland version of Tinker Bell from a book he'd bought for…

Never mind who he'd bought it for. He'd come to Kane's Crossing to forget about it.

They headed toward the patrol car, a gas-guzzling white Chevy behemoth that had seen better years.

"Lovely. Do I get the back seat," she asked, a hint of laughter in her voice, "where all the criminals languish?"

He held open the passenger's side front door in answer. She slid in, all grace and smooth curves. Years ago, she would've filled the definition of "coltish," but now, the term seemed outgrown.

Sam took his place behind the steering wheel. The occasional beep and burst of static from the police radio was the only sound as he tamped down his urge to look at her again. Another glance at Ashlyn Spencer would frustrate him, make him want things he didn't have a prayer of finding.

After he guided the car onto the silent country

road, he saw Ashlyn lean her head back against the headrest.

Suddenly he was much too aware of her scent, a combination of innocence—almonds, honey and cream. Something in his chest tightened, almost sputtered to life then died.

"So, do you want to explain this lionhearted quest of yours?" he asked, filling in the blank spaces of their conversation.

She hesitated, then lifted up her hands in a what-the-heck movement. "It's all pretty complicated, but…" She turned to face him, still resting her head. "Do you remember, years ago, when my family owned just about everything in town?"

He remembered with sharp clarity. "Yeah. I don't think your brother ever let *my* family forget."

Especially after the way Chad Spencer had treated Nick's wife, Meg, like a pleasure toy. Rumor had it that Chad had gotten Meg pregnant after making her think he loved her. That's when Nick had stepped in, claiming the resulting twins as his own children.

"Obviously you've talked with Nick," said Ashlyn, a faint smile lighting her face. "He really gave it to Chad good by buying those businesses and turning them over to those families in need. And my brother deserved it, even if I ended up feeling pretty sorry for him in the end. It's not easy having everything that matters taken away from you."

Everything that mattered: his parents, his wife…

"Go on." He relaxed his grip on the steering wheel, relieving the tight white of his knuckles, wondering why Ashlyn was still smiling. Could it be that she disagreed with how the Spencers had ruled over Kane's Crossing? Even when Sam had lived here, the town gossips had whispered that she ran around town, causing mischief, just to get back at her family for their zealous ways.

Sam didn't understand the concept, but it sure intrigued him.

Ashlyn continued. "To make a long story short, my family aims to get back all that they've lost. And I don't care to return to those days when the Spencers ruled."

Puzzlement shaped Sam's frown. "Why do you cause so much trouble for that family of yours?"

She clipped a laugh. "If you'd talked to Sheriff Carson before he died, he would've told you that I make mischief a habit. Simple as that."

Sam knew there was something more to it, but he doubted she'd reveal her intentions to him.

"At any rate," she said, "I can't stand the way some people in this town treat the Spencers like the second coming. And I don't like how my family feels the need to own people in return." She sat up, emphasizing the gravity of her explanation. "I'll do almost anything to discourage this football-hero worship, this money-god thrall that my brother and father have encouraged."

Sam wondered how her family felt about her protests. Funny, but he'd never looked at Ashlyn the way he had at Chad or her father Horatio Spencer. She'd always seemed to isolate herself. He'd never realized it until now, probably because he hadn't cared enough to bother.

Ashlyn asked, "You know that we own the toy factory again?"

That razor sting assaulted his soul once more. "I'd heard about it." Even if he'd moved back to

Kane's Crossing merely two months ago, folks had made sure he was caught up on all the gossip he'd missed—old and new.

"I have a bad feeling that my father's not down for the count. He'll take over everything again, and then Kane's Crossing is back to the dark ages."

Sam shook his head. "What about the citizens who own the properties now? I don't think they'll let that happen."

He could feel Ashlyn's appraisal of him, and he wondered if she knew why he'd come back to town after slinking away seven years ago, following his parents' deaths.

"It doesn't matter if the 'new regime' wants it or not. My father will be back in the game, Sheriff, buying all the properties he lost. He can't stand the lack of power." She clipped a laugh. "I wonder what my ancient granddad would say about all this. Founder of the town, the great Kane Spencer. You know he wanted Kane's Crossing to be a communal area, right?"

"I didn't know." Sam leaned one elbow on the armrest, using the other to palm the steering wheel around a sharp corner. *Casual. Be casual about this Spencer talk.* "Then I guess I'll be out of a job when your dad stretches his mighty muscles again."

"He'd get you fired in a second flat," she said in her colorfully blunt manner. "My family certainly holds no love for yours."

The word "love" caught in the air, and Sam just let it hang, knowing it would always be out of his reach.

He cleared his throat. "Speaking of tender feelings, because I know how much your brother loves mine, how is Chad?''

Ashlyn's voice seemed drained of its amused energy. ''He's hardly changed since you played football in high school. Still in Switzerland, married to a very forgiving wife. Coming back someday, I'm sure.''

Again, Sam thought about the rumors concerning Chad and Meg Cassidy. But that was tired news in Kane's Crossing. His brother ignored it, and Sam did, as well.

''So,'' she continued, switching the subject. ''I know I asked before, but why *did* you decide to come back to town? I heard you lived in D.C.''

The new conversational topic put him on guard, not only because she'd done it so jarringly, but because he was doing his best to forget about the past.

Flashes of crying children, an explosion lighting their eyes, haunted him. Echoes of screeching tires racked his brain.

''It was time for a change,'' he answered gruffly.

And she didn't push it. She must have sensed his disquietude, because she shifted her position, turning to stare out the window at the passing night. A closed-down filling station and gnarled trees streaked past, all a part of the shaded world that probably held a lot more colors and excitement for her than it did for him.

Ashlyn watched the world go by. Kane's Crossing and the town's *Saturday Evening Post* ambience could have fooled anyone with its innocence—the pristine picket fences, the daisy-petaled flower gardens, the creaking porch swings moaning about darker stories underneath their perfect facades.

The sheriff was right. It was time for a change.

But she'd never be brave enough to take a chance, to move out of her big, expensive house to explore everything outside her gates.

It was safer at home, with her own wing of the mansion, her own studio where she could create sculptures and design jewelry without anyone to tell her it was second-rate or useless. Her self-esteem wasn't ready to face the big, bad world. Besides, she couldn't leave her mother, not with the way she begged her only daughter to stay by her bedside, to help her get through countless illnesses.

Sometimes Ashlyn disgusted herself. Yeah, she was Ms. Muscle when it came to tearing down signs welcoming her brother home when he'd last returned from Europe. Yet, she didn't have the guts to admit that she wanted to help someone in need. Someone like Emma Trainor.

If she had any gumption whatsoever, she'd tell her father how much it hurt every time she came in second place to Chad. Every time he glowed when he introduced the favorite son. Every time his face fell when he introduced her, if he bothered.

Stewing about it wouldn't help. She'd known that for years. That's why she'd gotten into the habit of ingratiating herself with the townsfolk by poking fun at her family's royal image, cracking jokes with the old men on the general store porch while sipping bottled sodas, running with her girlfriends in the nearby creek with her dress hiked over her knees. All so very un-Spencer-like.

What they didn't know is how the flippancy had left her feeling a little dead inside.

"Miss Spencer?"

Sam. Sam Reno. She hadn't forgotten he was in the same car with her. And how could she forget, with his woodsy cologne faintly lingering in the air? A mix of freshly fallen leaves and spice mingling to disturb her thoughts.

"You can call me Ashlyn," she said, still facing the window, looking to her heart's content at his reflection. She slowly turned to face him, cuddling into the seat, seeing if he reacted to her movements.

Of course he didn't. Had his expression always been so stony, so devoid of animation?

She sat up a little straighter, game lost. At least she'd get a response from her father tonight, whether or not it was for the best.

He bit back his words with the tightening of his mouth, and she thought about how much moving to D.C. had changed him. His Doc Martens were too new, hadn't been broken in just yet. The same went for his clean lawman-brown jacket, his unfaded blue jeans. He looked like a city boy who'd forgotten the small town part of himself.

Through the windshield she caught sight of the Reno Center for Children as it whizzed by, lights out for the night. Then they pulled up to the sheriff's office, where the lamp was always burning.

He set the brake on the car and cut the ignition, turning to shoot a miffed gaze her way. And, in the car's dim light, she saw what he'd been hiding at Emma Trainor's.

Eyes the dead-hazel shade of desolation, like the muted colors of a predawn day when nothing stirs, nothing lives.

Sam Reno was hurting, no doubt about it.

Chapter Two

In the sterile light of the sheriff's office, Ashlyn noticed that Sam echoed the faded colors of a Remington painting, as well—the dusty oranges, browns and blues that spoke of still life and times gone by.

He led her to a seat in front of his hardwood desk, the top resembling a desert landscape with a minimum of papers and clutter. Well, if she had a desk in this place, it'd look like that, too, she supposed. All the sheriff of Kane's Crossing usually did was baby-sit drunks and chase around Spencer's wayward daughter anyway. The town hadn't seen any major action since... Her heart took a swan dive.

Since Sam's father had died in her family's factory.

As he sat at his desk and shucked off the jacket, she noticed that his badge had rusted around the edges.

He leaned back in his chair, propping his boots on the desk, reclining his head into his hands, surveying her with detachment. "Ashlyn Spencer, I don't know what the hell to do with you. Trespassing is illegal, no matter how honorable your intentions are."

She started to correct his assumption about her being a good person, but was cut off.

"Lock her up," rasped an inebriated entity from around the corner and in the back, where the holding cells were kept.

Ashlyn recognized the voice. "Not your business, Junior."

From the deputy's desk, the scanner came to life, putting in its two cents with an explosion of static.

Unfazed, Sam kept his gaze on Ashlyn. "I guess I could put you behind bars with Junior Crabbe, just for the fun of it."

She couldn't help her tart smile. "Definitely my idea of Shangri-la, Sheriff."

Junior Crabbe and his absent Siamese trouble twin, Sonny Jenks, had hung around her brother in their younger years. They were the bane of every peace-loving citizen's existence with their frequent drinking, brawling and carousing.

Problem was, she thought the sheriff just might put her in a cell with Junior. For fun. To teach her a lesson. To make up for the loss of Sam's father. Whatever the reason, she deserved it for her stubbornness.

Would that ever blow her father's top.

A whoosh of frigid air shivered over her back as the door burst open. She turned to see the new deputy, Gary Joanson, struggle in under the weight of another drunk, Sonny Jenks.

Gary's voice reflected his strain. "Evenin', Ashlyn. Sheriff."

"Joanson," said the sheriff, nodding a greeting, still eyeing his own problem for the night.

Gary, just a speck of a man, dragged the burly Sonny Jenks down the hall, where a happy Junior Crabbe's rebel yell greeted his buddy. Cries of "Traitor!" preceded the clank of jail bars, reflecting how Gary had befriended Nick Cassidy last year and turned against his bully-brained cronies.

Ashlyn was growing nervous under the sheriff's stare. She absently fingered her necklace, a piece of her own creation that, at times, pricked her skin with the edges of its incomplete circles.

"So," she said, wishing she could relieve the tension that had settled over the room, "aren't you glad to be back in Kane's Crossing?"

His face was expressionless. "Some days more than others."

Ashlyn slid her elbows onto the desk, one hand nestled under her chin as she smiled at him. "From what I hear, Meg Cassidy is making a lot of her blueberry 'boyfriend' pies over at the bakery."

"Meaning what?" He lowered his arms, sat forward in his chair.

Tread carefully. She didn't know him well enough to be flirting like this, but what did she have to lose? Maybe she could even talk her way out of trouble if she said the right words. "You know your sister-in-law and all the gossip about her baking. Eat an angel food cake of hers, you'll get married. Eat her chocolate cake, you'll get pregnant. I'm just saying she's been making a lot of blueberry pies since you came to town.''

The sheriff didn't even bother to comment, just suddenly became very preoccupied with a slim pile of papers on the corner of his desk. "How thick is your file here in the sheriff's office, Ashlyn?''

''Pretty huge.'' Maybe some flattery would be useful right about now. ''At any rate, since you became sheriff, women have been experiencing all sorts of emergencies in town, haven't they? False alarms, cookies that need to be eaten...''

His face got ruddy at this comment. Ashlyn decided to lean back in her chair, to put a cork in the cake conversation. This was obviously not a man who preened under the onslaught of compliments.

She recalled when his foster brother, Nick, had first come back to town, how he'd rarely smiled, either. But Meg, his wife, sure had him smiling now. Nick had fallen in love with Meg's surefire optimism and sense of self-worth. They were the happiest married people Ashlyn had ever seen.

She watched Sheriff Reno simmer down as he stood and ambled to the file cabinet. Ever so slowly, as if he had all the time in the world at his disposal, he thumbed through the manila folders, retrieving a *War and Peace*-thick collection. He tossed it onto the desk, the file thumping in her ears like a slap upside the head.

''Mine?'' she asked, pointing at the folder.

''All fifty pounds of it. I have to admire your perseverance, I suppose.''

She poked at it, remembering the contents without even having to look. Wait until he saw how idiot-stupid she could be. When it came to making her father angry, she was a very creative camper. Everything from decorating the factory's outside wall with pictures symbolizing workers' rights, to hiring a neighboring county's high school band to march in Spencer High's homecoming parade playing Twisted Sister's "We're Not Gonna Take It." Unfortunately, Horatio Spencer had appreciated none of this.

As she looked into Sam Reno's lifeless gaze, she saw a reflection, a young girl who needed to grow up, to let go of this bitterness she'd lived with since the age of seven, to get past her "bad girl" reputation and make a new life for herself.

She sat back in her chair, hands folded in her lap, head down. "I won't make your job harder than it needs to be."

"Thank you," he said, his voice wry enough to make her wonder if he was kidding.

She glanced at him, but he was still expressionless.

He continued. "Town pride isn't a bad thing to have, Miss Spencer."

Guffaws ricocheted through the holding cell, where Junior and Sonny were obviously listening.

"Yeah, Ashlyn, town pride!"

"Be a good neighbor! Come on back here and—"

A door slammed, and Gary Joanson's tinny voice rose above the taunts, quieting the drunks.

The sheriff shook his head, taking a step nearer to her. "Sorry about that."

"No, you're right," said Ashlyn. His thigh just about brushed her arm, and her skin actually buzzed from the almost-contact. "No more games, Sheriff. I've turned over a new leaf."

"Sounds sincere enough."

She met his gaze and almost fell into the bottomless depths of his eyes. What had happened in life to make him so sad? "Not to say I won't still have my fun, you understand."

He merely raised his brows.

"What I mean," she added, her protective shield of tough talk rising to the surface, "is that we come from utterly different places. This is my time to be carefree. You're Generation X and I'm Generation Why-Me…"

What was she trying to say? His stare, his *brooding,* was tangling her thoughts. Great, now she felt even younger, even more stupid.

When she looked at him again, a ghost of a smile lit over his mouth. A slanted grin, just as rusty as his badge. She wanted to use her fingertips to brush over his full lower lip, to test its softness.

Admit it, she thought. You've been dying to touch him since he hauled you away from Emma Trainor's porch.

Ashlyn sighed out loud, grinning in a heated flush when she caught the sheriff's still-cocked brow. "At any rate, you have my word. No more trouble."

Deputy Joanson walked into the office room, proud as a rooster. "How do, folks?"

Sam, smooth as still water, watched Ashlyn as he addressed his deputy. "You took my car tonight."

Ashlyn didn't break eye contact with Sam. Her pulse thudded in her ears, Gary Joanson's voice becoming nothing but background chatter.

"I thought you wouldn't mind—"

"—I mind."

Gary stepped into Ashlyn's view, dwarfed next to Sam Reno's sturdy frame. "I kinda like the Bronco, Sam."

Slowly, Sam turned to Gary, who took an unsteady step backward.

"Okay," said the deputy. "I'll take the grandma car."

That done, Gary tipped his cop hat to Ashlyn. "I was wondering when you'd make your first trip here, Ashlyn. What were you up to?"

She had the grace to look ashamed. "It depends on your point of view, I suppose."

"Isn't that always the case with you?" Gary slapped his knee in mirth. "Sheriff Carson would've been beet red by now."

Gary addressed Sam, who'd returned to staring at Ashlyn dispassionately. "This gal used to be a real firecracker, Sam. Before you hired me on, the other deputies would talk about how she kept Sheriff Carson busy and blowin' steam. Did ya decorate the town with some jokes tonight, Ashlyn?"

She kept her tongue. This night was becoming more humiliating by the second, but she wouldn't lose her cool in front of Sheriff Reno. She'd never let anyone—especially this man—know that she was crying inside. When people laughed at her jokes they were laughing at her and her family.

Sometimes it hurt to be laughed at.

"Deputy, do you have work to do?" asked Sam.

Gary hesitated, then, slump-shouldered, sat at the scanner desk, shuffling through papers.

Ashlyn heard Sam move closer to her again, felt

him looming over her. The breath caught in her throat.

"Up, Ashlyn," he said softly, his drawl lazing over her skin with the warmth of slow molasses.

She stood, almost body to body, eyes at the level of his corded throat. She'd always been considered a tall girl, gawky as a forest creature, all elbows and knees, but standing next to Sam Reno made her feel as if she were a normal person. As if she didn't stand out in a crowd.

He took her elbow, walking her near the door. When he let go, she wanted to seize his hand and put it right back. She didn't mind that her knees were turning to liquid, that she was all but clawing for breath inside.

After a pause, Sam took a step backward. He lifted up a finger, a wall between them. "I don't want to be called out on account of your wild schemes."

"I'll do my best to keep to myself, Sheriff." No more charitable gestures, no more *caring*. Nobody would believe her capable of it anyway.

"My name's Sam," he said, shrugging one wide shoulder. "Just…call me Sam."

She didn't want to leave, to go back to her house where she'd spend the night in her own lonely wing of the Spencer mansion, listening to sounds outside their sculpted iron gates.

It was sad, really. Emma Trainor had made it more than clear: Ashlyn wasn't welcome in Kane's Crossing. Those gates would help to shield her, to keep her from reaching out again.

While she was searching for words, he spoke.

"It's good to see a Spencer doing the right thing. I think Emma was thankful for your help."

Ashlyn had done her share of Spencer bashing, but his statement felt like a personal affront. "Some of us Spencers have a bit of honor."

Sam's hands rested on his lean hips. "That's not what I wanted to say."

"What did you intend?"

She noticed the slow simmer of his temper in the tensing of his fingers on his hips. "Let's forget it before I say something we both don't want to hear."

"Anything you say won't exactly be a news flash, *Sam.* Just go for it."

"Nothing." Dead, empty eyes, void of fight.

"Heck." She shrugged, wanting to get their differences out in the open. "Why don't I do it? The Spencers are a greedy lot. Stingy, monstrous, ugly. Is that it?"

He stayed silent.

How could she explain her flash of anger without seeming illogical? How could she make sense of the idea that she was the only one allowed to criticize her family? When she did it, it didn't hurt as much.

"I think it's time for you to leave, Ashlyn."

In the background, Deputy Joanson cleared his throat. Ashlyn attempted to rein in her temper.

"I know, Sheriff, that having your father killed at my family's factory won't make us best friends." There. She'd said it. Put it out there for Sam to handle any way he wanted.

Finally, something exploded in his eyes. His jaw tight, he said, "You don't want to know how much hate I hold for your family. If I were you, I'd just walk through the door."

He jerked his head toward the exit. "Joanson, drive her home."

She said, "My car's at Locksley Field. I can take it from there."

But he was already moving toward the jail cells, oblivious to her voice. She watched him leave, shame catching in her throat.

She hadn't gotten the chance to tell him how sorry she was about his parents.

But it didn't make much of a difference. He probably wouldn't listen anyway.

To Sam, this feeling of lingering guilt was much worse than any hangover he'd ever dealt with. And he'd nursed plenty of them following the weeks after he'd quit the District of Columbia Metropolitan Police Department in disgrace, the days after his wife's death.

As he listened to the blessed quiet of Junior and Sonny sleeping off their canned-beer binges, Sam wiped a hand over his face, regretting what he'd said to Ashlyn Spencer.

Of course, it was no big mystery that his father had been killed in the factory. Everyone in town knew it. Ten other people had died that day, as well. Worst part of it was, Horatio Spencer had blamed Sam's father for the deaths, but Sam knew better. His father had been talking about the grinding machinery, the wear and tear on the assembly line.

But any way you looked at it, Ashlyn wasn't responsible for those deaths. Putting her on the same level as her family wasn't fair.

Fairness. Justice. Words he didn't believe in anymore. His sense of faith in the world had died the night his wife, Mary, had been killed by a hit-and-run driver.

He'd quit his job a few weeks before the accident. So when his buddies from the D.C. police force had shown up on his doorstep, pity dragging down their expressions, he'd known something was very wrong. Sam even remembered the exact instant his soul had been sucked from his body by the news of her death. He remembered feeling a numbness slide into the place where he used to keep happiness in all the colors of a rainbow, the place he'd tried to fill with dreams of marriage and warmth.

Rainbows. He hadn't noticed one for a while, didn't even know if he could still recognize the different shades. But when he'd looked into Ashlyn's eyes tonight, he'd seen them—vibrant facets of blues, greens, violets—swirled together to create a glint of what heaven must look like.

Right, Sam. Just forget that she's a Spencer.

He couldn't forget the stark horror grimacing his mother's lips when she'd heard her husband had been caught in the Spenco Toy Factory machinery. Couldn't forget the quiet funeral she'd requested before she'd contracted a fatal case of pneumonia, joining her husband in death.

There were so many things he couldn't forget. Couldn't forgive.

Dammit, he'd come back to Kane's Crossing to erase his past. His parents were far enough in the land of memories that it shouldn't be tearing at him right now. All Sam wanted was to live the rest of his life in peace, in the presence of his foster brother, Nick, and his family.

Headlights flashed through the front office window, jerking Sam from his thoughts. Good thing, too. He'd never get any work done if he sank into a pool of emotion.

Deputy Joanson stuck his head in the door. "Sheriff?"

Sam tried not to seem as if he'd been mulling over useless memories again. "Yeah."

"Ashlyn Spencer? Well, I dropped her off at Locksley Field, but..."

By God. "What?"

"Well, I know the other deputies, before me, would've chased her down, but she's not too good at listening."

Sam stood, worried now. He realized his agitation and erased his mind. "What the hell did she do?"

"Oh." Gary stepped in the door, shrugged. "Nothing like that. Sorry to make you fret, Sheriff."

"I wasn't fretting."

"Right. So she said she had her car at the field, but she lied to me. Wouldn't get back in the grandma car. Said she'd rather freeze her patootie off than be caught dead in it again."

"She walked home?" Two degrees below red-nose weather and the blasted woman was taking a stroll? "I'll take care of it."

Gary shuffled his feet. "Sorry I couldn't tackle her like the other deputies would've. But she's a lady."

"Appreciate it, Joanson." Sam grabbed his coat and clutched the Bronco keys. And he thought he'd only have to deal with drunks as Kane's Crossing's sheriff. Ashlyn would obviously make him earn his paycheck.

"I know, I told her." Gary rattled on, blocking

Sam in his bid to provide more information. "Women-folk shouldn't be walking alone. Especially during April Fool's with the high school boys roaming around."

Sam almost laughed at his deputy's concern. Maybe Joanson should visit Washington, D.C., on a normal night. That'd give the guy nightmares for sure.

Still, the idea of Ashlyn walking home alone made him cringe. Any number of things could happen to a woman strolling by herself on a country road. Things he didn't want to think about.

"Besides," added Gary, "her daddy'll kill you if something happens to her."

"I wasn't put here to please Horatio Spencer," Sam said, shutting the door on Gary's answer.

The cold air nipped at his skin, and he thought of Ashlyn's thin, fashionable red sweater and ankle-skimming pants. What was going through her mind?

He settled himself into the Bronco, easing the vehicle onto the road again. Ashlyn Spencer—a synonym for trouble, if there ever was one.

He cruised to the outskirts of town, near the Spencer mansion, intending to backtrack from there to Locksley Field. When a flash of red sweater filtered into his headlight view, he slowed to a near stop, putting down the window to talk with Ashlyn.

She kept going, barely glancing at him, forcing him to do a U-turn and roll down the passenger window.

"Get in before I lasso you in."

Her walk was easy, swivel-hipped, casual. As if she were enjoying a sunny afternoon, parasol tipped over her head, fountains splashing in the background.

"I'm fine, Sheriff Sam."

He kept his silence, knowing words couldn't approach where his anger was leading him.

She seemed to catch his frustration, stopped, tilted her head. "I'm sorry for what happened to your family."

His vision went dark for a moment. All he could do was nod, accepting her sentiment. He would've apologized to her for his sharp attitude in the office, but he found it hard to speak with his throat burning as sorely as it was.

Damned wimp. Since when did he get so emotional?

He put the Bronco in neutral, pulled the emergency brake, slid over to open the door and extended a hand to help her into the vehicle. An eternity seemed to pass before she accepted, blazing his skin with the touch of hers.

Wasting no time once she was inside, he retreated back to his side of the car, angry at his body's reaction to her soft skin, her colorful eyes, her sweetheart smile.

Dammit.

He started up the car, drove a little faster than necessary in the hope of getting her away from him.

The police scanner did the talking for them, bits and pieces of static, beeps and Deputy Joanson's monotone saying, "Testing, testing…" He really needed to hire that dispatcher. As soon as possible, too.

It was no use thinking about the job. He was much too aware of her honey-and-almond scent, the way her hair stuck out at interesting angles, making her seem as though she'd just tumbled out of bed. It was a long drive all right.

After what seemed like generations later, they pulled up to the Spencer mansion. Normally, its thunderous iron gates were like muscle-bound arms crossed to the rest of the world. But tonight the gates were open.

He and Ashlyn exchanged looks, noting the oddity.

The engine purred as Sam hesitated, peering up the stretch of driveway, past the fortress of pines— trees that blocked the brick Colonial-style mansion from gawkers, those unworthy enough to happen upon the Spencers' seclusion.

He started to turn the steering wheel, aiming for the driveway.

Ashlyn reached out, her fingers clutching his biceps. They remained for a beat too long, lazily sketching down the length of his forearm as she absently peeked out the window at her grandiose home. He wasn't sure she knew what she was doing, touching him like this, leaving a trail of dangerous fire that had spread from his arm to his stomach.

"I'll bet my father's waiting for me," she said.

The words sounded ominous because Sam thought maybe Horatio Spencer was waiting for him, too. Waiting to blast him a glare he usually reserved for Sam's foster brother, the one who'd purchased the all-important businesses from under the Spencers' noses.

It didn't matter that Nick had been helping needful families by giving them houses and businesses with money from his self-constructed fortune. Horatio Spencer looked upon the whole episode as a young man's revenge against Chad, his son. The son who'd framed a teenage Nick for a crime he hadn't committed.

Sam held back a grimace, welcoming this chance to greet Horatio.

Ashlyn's hand left his skin, traveling from his arm to her neck, toying with the necklace she wore. It was a chunk of ordinary gravel, surrounded by gleaming silver half circles. He wondered why someone as rich as Ashlyn Spencer wasn't wearing emeralds or sapphires to go with the shine of her eyes.

He couldn't help asking about the charm. "Is your talisman strong enough to get you out of trouble?"

She started, maybe just realizing that she'd been rubbing it as if it were Aladdin's lamp. "I've got my own strength."

Shut out, as he'd done to her so many times tonight. "Right."

Her smile was wistful. "It's nothing, anyway. Just my albatross."

He cocked his brow, not knowing what to say. Instead, they both returned their attention to the open gates.

"Let's go," he said.

Chapter Three

Ashlyn couldn't believe Sam had cared enough to hunt her down and drive her home.

But, she told herself, don't read too much into it. He's the sheriff. He protects people.

Her hand still tingled from when she'd touched his muscled arm—tingles powered by a little girl's dreams. If Horatio Spencer saw her in this car with someone who could be considered the family enemy, she'd have hell to pay. Even Ashlyn's mother wasn't too fond of the Renos and their foster son, Nick Cassidy.

Ashlyn still recalled the day she'd come home from Meg and Nick's wedding, having served as an impromptu maid-of-honor. They'd caught her hanging out with the old men from the general store, rocking on the porch, exchanging salty jokes and laughter. She'd been oddly touched when Meg had hopped from Nick's beat-up truck, five-month-pregnant tummy and all, to ask her to stand up for their union. Ashlyn had taken great pride in picking wildflowers for the bridal bouquet, in standing next to Meg at the altar while they'd exchanged vows.

She'd mattered to someone. She'd played a positive part in Meg and Nick's happiness.

But when her mother had caught wind of the gossip, she'd all but keeled over. Ashlyn didn't even want to remember what her father had said.

Sam floored the gas pedal, and Ashlyn grabbed the door handle. The Bronco flew up the driveway.

While trees swished by, Ashlyn tried to calm herself, hoping that she'd been wrong about her father being home. Maybe he was still at work, practicing his usual late-night hours.

They pulled onto the circular path that looped in front of the white doors and columns of her home. No one stood outside. Ashlyn breathed a sigh of relief, but stopped short when her gaze traveled to the second story.

Framed by a window, her mother's silhouette stood sentinel, hand raised to her mouth. Ashlyn could imagine a cough racking Edwina Spencer's body and the pills she would take to make her ailments disappear. Until the next sickness came along. And the next.

Her mother's shadow seemed all the more desolate due to the two nearly deserted mansion wings spanning either side of her. All the windows reflected darkness, silence.

After Ashlyn left Sam, she'd shuffle to her room in one of those wings, alone, listening to the wind whistling through the halls, wondering if she'd ever have the courage or confidence to leave the only place she felt comfortable being a Spencer.

Sam pulled up to the doorway, stopping the vehicle. He watched her mother's shadow, too, perhaps wishing *he* had a family to come home to. Or maybe Ashlyn was being overly fanciful, interpreting his softened gaze as more than it was.

His mouth turned up in a slight smile as Ashlyn realized she was staring again.

He said, "Could you do me a favor next time and drive a car at night? Not even Kane's Crossing is one-hundred percent safe."

Yet, right now, she felt protected, oddly secure, with him. "Sheriff Sam, your big-city fears are showing."

"Better safe than sorry." He waited for her to leave, idling the engine.

It was hard for her to open the car door, step out onto the cold asphalt driveway. Staying with Sam would've felt much better.

She said, "I almost wish you could come in, enjoy a spot of tea, engage in some civilized conversation, you know."

Sam actually laughed, sounding more like a creaking hinge in a dark room than anything. But it was a start.

"Maybe in Bizarro World." He paused. "Not that Kane's Crossing is so much different."

Finally, a bit of levity from the man. Ashlyn knew he had it in him. "Are you sure you don't want to try? I've got coffee, the aforementioned tea…" *Me*.

Yeah, right, she thought. As if tall, handsome, honorable Sam Reno would fall for her, the runt of a very distinguished litter.

Sam focused his attention on her mother's window again, a grin lingering as he shook his head.

Ashlyn followed his gaze, noticing how the velvet curtains moved back and forth, caught in the wake of her mother's disappearance.

Was her father home? How long would it be before he burst through the front door, engaging Sam in the inevitable confrontation between Spencer and Reno?

While she weighed the comfort of being with Sam against the desire to defend him from anguish, she felt a light touch brush over the hair at the nape of her neck. Her skin goose-bumped, making her feel dizzy, mystified.

She turned back to Sam, catching him staring straight ahead, one hand resting against his door, one fisting the steering wheel.

Had the contact been her imagination? If she didn't know any better, she'd have guessed that he'd run his finger over her hair, just like a whisper of air over leaves.

No, this was crazy. Sam had too much self-control for games like that.

Maybe she was tired, her mind playing mean tricks on her.

She sighed. "Thanks for going easy on me tonight."

"'Easy' doesn't describe you, Ashlyn." Again, that ghost of a grin slanted his lips.

Now she really needed to leave, before she curled up next to him, light as a wisp of smoke, to feel the security of his arms.

She opened the car door, grinning at him. "Good

riddance'' was probably pin-balling through his thoughts, and she couldn't blame him in the least.

''Good night,'' she said softly.

He lifted a hand, gesturing a laconic farewell.

Typical Sam Reno. She walked up the stone stairway, lined by spring's newest azaleas, their pink blooms reflecting her attitude. He'd smiled, laughed. And the responses made her giddy, layering hope upon hope in her soul.

What if…?

As she turned around to catch a last glimpse, he lightly shut the door and drove away, the Bronco's red taillamps streaking down her driveway, red as Cupid's kisses.

As untouchable as Sam himself.

Sam couldn't believe he'd touched her hair.

Damn him, he'd actually reached out as she'd turned away from him, wisping his finger through one of her short, sandy locks.

He gritted his jaw, guiding the Bronco down the driveway. What had come over him?

They'd been sitting in the car, a typical goodnight-to-you drop-off when she'd smiled at him with all the power of midday sunshine. Then she'd said something cute, something flippant enough to divert his attention from the upstairs-window shadow, lording it over the fancy Spencer mansion and its twinkling porch lights.

Another house that greed had built.

And, dammit, he'd seen enough greed in Washington, D.C., to last him five lifetimes.

Kids, walking home from school, when…

Sam shut his mind's eye to the sight, punching away the memories.

Instead, he watched his headlights suffuse the pine trees, the willow by the massive Spencer gates.

He'd touched her hair, and it had felt just as soft as he'd imagined. Sam used to touch Mary's hair, too. He'd done it to reassure her, done it when he'd wanted her to look at him. It had always been an absent gesture, borne of the need for comfort.

When he'd reached out to Ashlyn, he hadn't even been thinking straight; he'd merely been reacting to the welcome happiness their banter had induced.

What? *Happiness?*

Sam turned on to the country road, lining up the Bronco in his lane to adjust to an oncoming car. A Mercedes.

He accelerated just as Horatio Spencer slowed down, turning into his driveway. Sam caught a slow-motion glimpse of the man's miffed glance, the startled moment of recognition as Horatio saw the sheriff's vehicle.

Sam steadied his pulse, pulling the Bronco away from the mansion. He'd have to come face-to-face with the man someday. Confront his family's demons head-on.

But in the meantime, Sam would do well to avoid Ashlyn Spencer. He didn't need another woman in his life, especially after what he'd done to lose his wife. He didn't need the pain.

Sam drove into darkness, into the dead zone, once again feeling a dull stillness as it settled around his body.

And around his heart.

* * *

Ashlyn stepped inside the mansion, the Italian-marbled foyer seeming cold and lifeless.

She thought of going to the kitchen to grab a few leftovers for a late dinner, but decided she was too excited to be hungry. Instead, she wandered to the antique Baltimore secretary leaning against the wall, reaching inside to retrieve the mail that the downstairs maid had dropped off.

Catalogs, junk ads, wastes of good paper. Heck, why couldn't she even pay proper attention to her mail?

The front door opened, and she felt him. Her father, watching her from behind.

His voice, rough as rocks crashing together in the black of a cave, said, "It wasn't bad enough when you played bridesmaid to the Cassidys, was it? Now you're sleeping with the enemy."

"Hello, Father," she said, making sure her tone was unaffected. She turned around, grinning her ain't-I-sweet-as-sugar smile.

He seemed to fill the door frame with his wiry stance, encased by a business suit even this late at night. She'd gotten her height from him, and she shuddered to think what else she might've inherited.

His hair, black-and-white as marbled stone, all but stood on end. As he stepped inside, Ashlyn could've sworn she saw something like concern tumble through his dark eyes, but then—poof!—it disappeared.

"What circus act of yours brought the sheriff to our doorstep?" asked her father.

His verbal barb was unfair, and he should've known it. Ashlyn hadn't gotten under the law's skin since her brother Chad had come home last year.

And even then, she hadn't done anything serious—
just a practical joke concerning Chad's shoes and
some horse pucky in a paper bag.

She reached up to fidget with her necklace.

Memories flashed through her head: gravel blinding her, dirt drying her mouth, her father's voice
announcing her second-place station in life. Right
behind Chad.

She dropped her hands to her sides, tilting her
head, grin turning to stone. "I was merely taking in
some fresh air, Father. There's not much to be had
at home."

"You missed dinner, Ashlyn."

So she had. "I'll grab something from the
kitchen."

Her father frowned. "Eugene Hampton was here.
Did you or did you not remember you were to meet
him tonight?"

Oh, brother. Another one of her father's blind date
proposals. Every month held another possibility of
some Harvard School of Business graduate coming
to dinner to meet Ashlyn, and, predictably, she always did her best to sabotage any hope on their part.

It struck her that maybe she was too good at ru-
ining relationships.

"Sorry, Father. Maybe next time?"

"And there will be a next time," he said, his
voice following her into the foyer. His statement
echoed, racing along the spiral stairway that led to
a higher floor. "I've invited Eugene to the Spenco
Toy Factory opening picnic next weekend, so mind
that you're there."

Ashlyn crossed her arms, met his stare head-on.
"Let's be honest. These things never work out. I

can't believe that, after five years, you're still trying to set me up with the man you believe is Mr. Right for the Money.''

''You saw what happened when that whelp Nick Cassidy came in and took a bite of our holdings. I'd like your future to be secure.'' Her father shut the front door behind him, blocking out the night sounds.

The Cassidy name leveled an uncomfortable silence between them, as if it were a physical reminder of Chad framing Nick for her own brother's crime. ''Please don't bother with my future, Dad.''

He stepped into her view, stern as the suit of armor decorating the entrance to his game room.

''Sorry. *Father.*''

''That's it for now.''

He hesitated, and Ashlyn knew he was dying to say something more about Sam Reno or his family before dismissing her altogether. She willed him to speak, but his hard, dark eyes erased the need.

She wondered how her father would react if she said Sam's name, allowing it to reverberate through the mansion's sterile halls. His name was already bouncing off the walls of her heart, every thump reminding her of a teenage boy who'd unwittingly encouraged a little girl's innocent crush. She still remembered how he'd smiled her way one lonely night—years and years ago—making her feel special. Wanted. Even for an anonymous moment.

Instead he said, ''See your mother before you retire, Ashlyn. She's worried.''

She's worried. If Chad had been out until the ghosting hour, if he'd been escorted home by the law, her father would've been frantic.

At least Ashlyn merited concern from her mother.

She tried to not let her shoulders droop as she climbed the stairs, sliding her hand along the polished cherrywood. She felt her father watching her, but she wouldn't peek down, wouldn't let him know that she was aware of his stare.

She moved past the wallpaper, its design showcasing half circles floating among lines and gild, the incomplete rings seemingly reaching out to connect with one another.

Her heart smarted as she glimpsed her red second-place horse show ribbons hidden behind Chad's treasure trove of State Championship football trophies and uniform jerseys as she passed the glass-encased trophy cabinet on the second-floor parlor.

Her mother's door revealed a crack of light around the edges. She usually didn't stay up so late.

Ashlyn knocked lightly and entered when urged to by a wispy, Southern-genteel voice.

The stench of medicines mixed with expensive perfume assailed her. "Hello, Mother."

Edwina Spencer shifted beneath the silken covers of her king-size bed, knocking over a glass pill jar. It clanked against other containers. "Ashlyn?" she slurred.

"It's me." She strolled to the nightstand, grabbing the empty jars on the way. She placed them amid half-filled atomizers and more prescription tubes. "Feeling better tonight?"

Her mother heaved a sigh, pushing back a thinning patch of blond hair from her faded blue eyes. Her brother looked more like their mother with her china-doll fragility.

"Oh, no, Lynnie. I'm awful, simply awful."

Ashlyn recalled the sight of her mother's shadow by the window, but didn't comment. "I'm sorry to hear that. Do you need me to get you anything?"

"Dear, that's what the maid is for. She'll fetch whatever I require."

She waited for the older woman to ask where Ashlyn had been tonight, but she knew her mother wouldn't say anything unless forced to. For as long as Ashlyn could remember, pills had helped Mrs. Spencer avoid life.

Instead, her mother played the guilt card. "I miss you when you're not here, Lynnie."

She'd heard these words time and again, especially when she'd been eighteen and ready to move out into the real world.

Ashlyn still recalled the new bedroom accessories she'd purchased with earnings from jewelry and sculptures she'd sold on the sly, the friends she'd made at college orientation day. But one well-thought guilt-trip from her mother had kept her home, out of the dorms, attending the local college instead.

"I'm so happy you care enough to stay with your poor mother. I don't know what I'd do without you."

Ashlyn tried not to cringe, tried not to think of what her life would be like if she had the courage to leave the mansion. Would she be able to get along with Sam Reno more easily if she distanced herself from her family?

"Maybe you should get some sleep, Mother."

Two bony, vein-webbed hands shot out to clamp onto Ashlyn's arms. "Don't leave me."

Ashlyn wondered what her mother had taken tonight. Valium?

She pulled back from the skeletal hands, played with her necklace. It seemed more like a collar and leash than jewelry right now. "I won't leave you."

The words felt like hands clutching her ankles, dragging her down into a dark hole that was cold and ragged enough to scrape off her fingernails as she grabbed for purchase.

"That's my girl. I'm so thankful for my Lynnie." And with that her thin-as-parchment eyelids fluttered shut, her frill-collared nightdress making Edwina Spencer seem even more breakable.

After a moment of collecting herself, Ashlyn left the room, embarking upon the lonely walk to her side of the mansion.

That night, in his box-littered kitchen, Sam stood in front of his open refrigerator, lit by its glaring bulb.

Damn the Spencers. Damn *him* for being unable to forget the past, the pain.

Part of him wanted to be back in D.C., away from the tangled mess of Kane's Crossing and all the history of his family. But he couldn't stand the thought of shuffling around the town house he'd once shared with his wife, reminding him of his shortcomings. That's partly why he'd moved in the first place.

Now, in his new home, it wasn't much better. He still hadn't unpacked his belongings. The rooms yawned with empty walls and the absence of furniture. He'd gone poking around the basement a time or two, before he'd officially accepted the sheriff's position, but Sam hadn't wanted to disturb the graveyard-like atmosphere of someone else's life, as represented by antique furniture and boxes filled with mementos.

The former owner had moved to a nursing home in Memphis, Tennessee, closer to his family. He'd left most of his belongings to the next occupant, obviously thinking they'd be of some use. Of course, if Sam could manage to adopt someone else's life, that might not be a bad thing. Maybe it was even a good idea, based on the mess he'd almost made tonight with Ashlyn.

Hell, why did he even care about it? Even if Ashlyn had stirred more heat into his body than he'd felt in years, that didn't mean squat. It was only lust—that hormone-driven Mack truck. Nothing to lose his head over.

Sam shifted, his jeans scratching the refrigerator door, as he peered at an army of beer bottles. Looked a lot like his days as a soldier, grouped together with his platoon of fighting machines, honing their discipline, dreaming of life beyond that short military stint.

After putting his days in the service behind him, Sam had gone back to college to earn a master's degree in criminal justice. He'd then returned home to spend time with his parents before devoting himself to a career in law enforcement.

He'd been visiting Kane's Crossing when his dad had been killed. Sam had done his best to take care of his mom in the aftermath, but it had been too little, too late.

After his mom's death, he'd headed to D.C. to fulfill his dream of becoming a cop, of getting married and living in peace.

Thoughts of his dead wife twisted his throat until it burned. He didn't want to think about her and their short-lived marriage. He couldn't stand to think about the death of his own soul.

Dammit. He'd made his choices. And now he needed to live with the consequences.

He looked at the beer again, the shimmer of glass reminding him of Ashlyn Spencer's lively gaze.

He needed to stop making bad choices.

Sam thrust shut the refrigerator door, the clink of the bottles mocking him with their glee.

On the other side of town, Ashlyn wandered from her art studio back to her bedroom. She had no patience for the paint-splattered canvas hideaway tonight. No tolerance for sitting still, running her fingers over shapeless metal, trying to conjure ideas that wouldn't leave the darkness of her mind for fear of failing. Even so, her hands desperately needed something to do.

She bent down, peeking beneath her bed. There it was, a web-shrouded memory book.

After pulling it out, she flipped open the yellowed pages, smiling when she came across a blue jeans' pocket from her first boyfriend, who'd torn it from his backside and given it to her on a whim. He'd moved from town the next month after the Spencers foreclosed on his family's home.

Dried flowers, watercolor paintings, journal entries, magazine clippings... Here it was.

The red ribbon.

Ashlyn clutched it, remembering how it had comforted her beneath the Spencer High football bleachers on that October night so long ago.

At seven years old, she'd hidden in the darkness, peeking through the slats of the seats, feeling locked in the shadows of her traumatic cave memories. Beneath the bleachers, she had safely tucked herself away, becoming invisible.

As she'd drawn pictures in the dirt with a discarded straw, she spied a tall, wiry silhouette—broad through the shoulders and lean in the hips—blocking the light of the locker room. The boy ambled nearer, to a cheerleader whom Ashlyn hadn't noticed leaning against a nearby water fountain.

Jo Ann Walters. Ashlyn had caught her breath, hoping that she'd grow up to look just like the head cheerleader, a girl even her stuck-up brother went silly over. She reminded Ashlyn of a princess in one of her Disney storybooks, all pink and slender, with a smile that glimmered with fairy dust.

Enthralled, Ashlyn had set down the straw, sniffed her runny nose and found a comfortable place to spy on her role model.

Even now, with the passage of years, Ashlyn could still see the light from the locker room as Jo Ann had fallen into the boy's arms.

They'd kissed hello and, afterward, the boy thrust a bunch of what looked like flowers at Jo Ann, who accepted them with a giggle.

It was the most romantic thing Ashlyn had ever seen. Her father never brought her mother anything, not even chocolates. They'd always ignored each other.

Ashlyn sighed, remembering how she'd wished that someday someone would look at her the way the boy had looked at Jo Ann.

She remembered cringing back into the shadows

as the couple began walking to the parking lot, passing her hiding place.

As if in slow motion, a ribbon had fluttered to the ground from the flower stems, a perfect circle, a shadow in the light.

She'd scuttled from her hiding place to retrieve it, running it between her fingers with something akin to awe. It was soft and silky, as red as a Valentine.

The boy must've heard her, because he turned around, light suffusing his face.

Sam Reno, one of her brother's football teammates.

She'd wanted to run back to her hiding place, to cower in shame. A silly ribbon. What would Sam think of her?

But he'd smiled. A crooked slant of a smile that had led to years of teenage dreaming for Ashlyn. No boy had ever lived up to it since.

Now Sam was back, and he probably couldn't stand the sight of her.

Ashlyn wandered to the window, and stared at the dim lights of Kane's Crossing in the near distance. The wooden window frames cast barlike shadows over her hands as she held up the ribbon to the moon, watching its circle imprint on the silvery light.

Somehow she felt like the world's most privileged prisoner.

Chapter Four

At the Spenco Toy Factory picnic, a slight chill rested beneath the brightness of a sunny April sky. A week had passed since Ashlyn's latest encounter with Sam Reno. A week filled with hard work on an inspired sculpture. A week void of trespassing and Sam Reno's glowering eyes.

Ashlyn tossed a Frisbee to a distant cousin she barely knew. The thirteen-year-old boy leaped up to retrieve it. Obviously, height graced only her branch of the family.

The cousin flipped the Frisbee back to Ashlyn, who plucked it from the air with ease. She glanced at her mother, who was swaddled in blankets and propped up in a comfortable chair. Ashlyn forced a wink, trying to convince her mother and herself that she wanted to be here.

It was downright odd, seeing one half of Factory

Bluff flanked by the Spencers and their followers, the other half boasting everyone who now owned the Spencers' old businesses. The "new regime," as her father liked to say.

Without seeming too obvious, Ashlyn peeked at that side of the bluff, noting that Sam's foster brother, Nick, and his family and friends reclined on multicolored blankets, while Sam Reno isolated himself on a swath of gray.

She tried to still her heart, convincing herself that it was pounding in her ears so loudly because of the exercise. The smart part of her knew better.

That silly, schoolgirl crush on Sam Reno still existed and was thriving under his return to Kane's Crossing.

A few of her girlfriends crossed to the middle of the field. "Hey, Ashlyn!" yelled one. "Get over here!"

Strange. She didn't see a chasm separating them. But, all the same, she knew it was there, dug out during years of town tension.

She winged the Frisbee back to her cousin, gave a tiny wave and moved to neutral ground. "Do my relatives scare you that much?"

Nell Cocanougher tucked back a strand of her strawberry-blond hair. "Just your dad. Say, we haven't seen you around lately. We heard you got busted by the sheriff last week."

Cheryl Perry, a short, ringleted blonde, interjected, "Not that it's anything new. But this sheriff's—"

Carmen Harvey cut in. "A babe!"

They all turned to stare directly at Sam. Ashlyn hid her face, hoping he hadn't noticed.

"Hey, girls. Be a little more obvious, why don't you."

Carmen raised her dark eyebrows. "Did he give you any slack for giving that money to Janey Trainor? I heard Emma held a shotgun on you."

Nell inserted her own view of the situation. "You'd think the woman would be bowing at Ashlyn's feet. Janey's doing real well in the hospital, thanks to that donation."

Great. The whole town knew about what she'd been doing at Emma Trainor's house that night.

As black-and-white-uniformed caterers started to serve the food, Ashlyn seized the opportunity to change the subject.

"Anyone care to join me here in limbo?" She gestured to the empty strip between the two camps.

The girls nodded and spread out their spring dresses as they sat on the grass. The caterers swooped right over to them, setting down plates of grapes, oranges and sliced apples with a light caramel dip.

"Appetizers," said Cheryl. "Don't you feel just like Cleopatra?"

"Say, Ashlyn," said Nell, "it's great hanging out with you. We always get great service."

It helped that her family was footing the bill for the festivities. In his eagerness to establish that he was back in the Kane's Crossing game, her father had gone overboard, inviting the entire town and decorating the grounds with kites to fly in the air, colorful banners, and life-size stuffed animals, to say nothing of the myriad games for the kids. Only Ashlyn knew that he'd borrowed money from their bank-industry relatives in Europe to make everyone think the Spencers were still rolling in dough.

But things weren't all bleak. Factory work was scheduled to start on Monday and, contrary to predictions, Horatio Spencer hadn't experienced any problems hiring his workers. Kane's Crossing would always have an underclass.

Ashlyn surreptitiously looked Sam's way. He'd been joined on his blanket by a beautiful woman and a young girl. Rachel Shane, she thought, envy nipping at her forced smile.

She tried to ignore Sam, but every time she saw Rachel lean next to him with her long, shiny, straight hair swinging near his nose, Ashlyn gritted her teeth.

Why had she cut her hair five years ago? Maybe Sam liked Rachel's flowing-angel look.

If so, she'd never catch up to the older woman. Not in hair, not in age or maturity.

Second place for life.

Just as she was in her family, with Chad always running first.

"Ooooh," whistled Carmen. "I think Ashlyn's got an itty-bitty crush."

"Please," said Ashlyn, mustering all the grace she could gather.

Cheryl nodded. "Can you imagine? A Reno and a Spencer? Daggone, Ashlyn, your family would string you up by the thumbs."

And that'd be only the first round of her punishment.

The peanut gallery known as Nell added her opinion. "If you're so disinterested, why are you staring at him?"

Ashlyn whipped her gaze back to their food. She snapped a grape from its stem and popped it into her mouth, buying time. Finally she said, "I'm looking at the cute Cassidy twins, you gossip."

Nobody had to say that Meg Cassidy's one-year-old children, Jake and Val, might just be her nephew and niece. She'd never breathe a word of it, either. She had too much respect for Meg. Sam's vibrant sister-in-law still owned the bakery on Main Street and also ran the Big Brother and Sister program at the Reno Center, which housed and educated hopeful foster children.

"Precious little babies," murmured one of the girls, suddenly paying a lot of attention to the food.

Ashlyn wondered what would happen if she crossed the invisible line to talk to Meg. After all, she'd been her bridesmaid at the wedding. It was, of course, all an accident that she'd been whiling away time at the general store when Meg and Nick had needed witnesses. But still, she felt that she'd contributed to their successful marriage. Even in some small way.

Meg caught her eye and waved. Ashlyn grinned back.

She peeked at Sam again while the girls were enthralled by the next course—salad with all the trimmings, on a lazy Susan.

She pushed aside her plate, watching how Sam leaned back on his elbows, his khaki shirt still as crisp and new as a cold frost. Rachel tossed back her head, laughing at something her daughter said as the little girl chucked a grape at a half-smiling Sam.

A fist of agony squeezed her heart as he tossed

the round fruit into the air and caught it in his mouth. Both females clapped at his antics.

Just never you mind, Ashlyn, she told herself. Eat your food and be the paradigm of good manners. Don't let them see that you care about the way he grins at that six-year-old girl. Don't let him know that you'd like to see him grinning in your direction, too.

Unwilling to allow her friends a modicum of insight as to how Sam and Rachel affected her, Ashlyn talked up a storm during the ensuing meal. She told the most charming jokes, keeping her pals in stitches while she tried to hold together her composure. She ate every last bite of the grilled shrimp, thrilled to the thyme-and-garlic kick of the roasted mixed mushrooms. She praised the asparagus niçoise, the red-wine vinegar and Dijon-mustard taste clinging to the roof of her mouth.

When Ashlyn and her friends had enjoyed their fill of peach-almond cake, they all sat back on the grass, hoping their stomachs weren't too misshapen from all the delicious food.

As the sun warmed Ashlyn's cheeks, she heard a stir in the distance. Prying open one eye, she saw that her father's most trusted employees were starting picnic games: sack races, a water-balloon toss, and a tug-of-war. Children from both sides of the field, without a thought to right or wrong, joined each other to play. The kids from the Reno Center had even lined up to participate, clapping their hands in anticipation.

Her impish spirit awoke with a start. She loved games.

But she'd probably look immature in Sam's jaded eyes.

Ashlyn leaned back on her elbows, resigned to looking *mature*.

"Oh, how cute," said Cheryl. "They're getting the Big Brothers and Sisters from the Reno Center to form tug-of-war teams with their kids."

Carmen sighed. "I thought of joining that program, you know. But Meg Cassidy seems to encourage couples to do it together, kind of like a pre-parent training thing. And we know that I never have a boyfriend who stays around long enough to enlist in a program that requires commitment."

"Hear, hear," said Nell.

Their words escaped Ashlyn's attention as she enjoyed the children's excitement. One boy in particular caught her eye.

He sat by himself, watching the Big Brothers and Sisters triple up with their kids. He cradled one hand in the palm of the other, a sunny smile on his dusky-skinned face.

Didn't he have anyone? The thought of him being rejected and all alone made Ashlyn want to cry. She couldn't imagine what it must be like to be orphaned.

She stood, brushed off her dress. Why should she start caring about other peoples' opinions anyway? "Tug-of-war sounds fun."

Nell laughed. "You've got to be kidding me. You and your little skirt in a kid's game. Get out the binoculars, all you males."

"It won't get to that point. Remember, I'm pretty good at games." She peeked out of the corner of her eye at Sam. It looked as if he was watching her, too. Adrenaline spiked her veins.

"Anyone else up for this?" she asked.

Her comrades shook their heads. Ashlyn shrugged and waved goodbye, wandering toward the lonely child.

As she approached, he smiled even wider. "Hi," he said, one hand still cupped by the other.

She felt even more sorry for him when she realized he couldn't have been more than eight. "Hey. Aren't you interested in some tug-of-war?"

Still grinning, he held up the hidden hand. It was a nub, round little fingertips sprouting out where long digits should've been.

A flash of shock kept her from saying anything. Oddly enough, she wanted to apologize for his lot in life, but that would be ridiculous. Instead, she made the most of the moment.

She held out her own hand, inviting him to shake it with the nub. "I'm Ashlyn Spencer. Pleased to meet you."

This time his Spaniel-brown eyes lit up, his wavy black hair lifting in the breeze. "I'm Taggert, but most folks call me Tag."

She knew that the kids at the Reno Center didn't usually have real last names, so she didn't ask. She wondered if Nick Cassidy, who'd founded the center in reaction to his own miserable foster experiences, knew what a gem this little guy was.

They shook hands, his skin soft and round in her cupped palm. It was hard to explain, but she felt a kinship with Tag. Maybe because, in his smile, she sensed the willingness to believe in magic. Or maybe it was the dignified way he handled being alone and ignored.

"Well, Tag, you seem pretty bored just sitting here. Are there any games that interest you?"

"Yeah. Tug-of-war." He stood up, a diminutive warrior. "Think we can find another person?"

Meg Cassidy walked up to them. Her curly, red hair was swept off her neck with a chiffon scarf. "Hi, Tag, Ashlyn. Don't tell me, Taggert, you're wrangling your new friend into some trouble."

"No, Mrs. Cassidy." His dusky skin flushed.

"Tag wants to play tug-of-war." Ashlyn widened her eyes at Meg, who didn't seem fazed by this announcement.

"Well," she said, her green gaze scanning the picnic grounds, "then you'll need another person."

She peered behind Ashlyn, crooking her finger at someone in a come-hither gesture.

Before he even arrived, Ashlyn knew whom Meg had summoned.

Sam Reno stood next to her, all woodsy-soap smell and muscled height. He robbed her of the ability to breathe correctly.

Over a week ago she might've dimpled at him and said something along the lines of, "So where's your sweet thing, Rachel Shane?" Today, in her mission to be more mature in his thirty-three-year-old eyes, she simply grinned.

His gaze flashed over her momentarily, without emotion, then turned to Tag. Ashlyn's smile felt frozen.

Of course he would ignore her. The last time she'd seen him he'd been high-tailing it down her driveway, beating the devil to get away from her.

Meg broke the awkwardness and introduced him to Tag. "Sam, we need a third party for tug-of-war. How about it?"

Most people in town were a little bit afraid of Meg Cassidy, not only because of her husband's money and power, but because she was known as the town "witch." She and her family lived in "the house on haunted hill," the one where everyone whistled as they walked past its looming gables and dark-wooded thunder.

Ashlyn rather liked the house. It had personality, and so did Meg. She wished Sam would borrow some of that animation from his sister-in-law.

Sam gruffly nodded his head toward Tag. "You any good at games?"

Tag jumped to his feet. "Yes, sir. Plenty good."

Sam still avoided her gaze. "Great. Then Ashlyn Spencer, here, won't have to make up for anything we lack."

She wondered if she should feel offended, but the comment had actually been sort of funny. And true.

"Well, Sheriff, games require a sense of humor. Are you sure you're up to it?"

He dragged his gaze over to her as if it were a heavy load. His hazel eyes held an amused glint among the boggy colors. Ashlyn wondered how many people had called him on his wry comments.

A grin flickered on his lips, sending a jolt through Ashlyn.

Tag scuttled between them, grabbing Ashlyn's wrist on his way to the rope. While she was pulled to the tug-of-war festivities, Ashlyn peered over her shoulder, still holding eye contact with Sam.

A heartbeat exploded between them, marking an endless second.

But Meg crushed the moment, pushing Sam forward, a smug smile on her lips. Ashlyn saw his mouth move in a muttered curse, and then he followed.

Sam grumbled under his breath. Never mind that tomorrow was the seventh anniversary of his father's death, which made all these festivities a travesty. Never mind that he was supposed to be on the job, patrolling this hotbed for ill feelings disguised as a picnic. He was going to play a rousing game of tug-of-war.

He told himself day in and day out that he didn't even like kids. Didn't want to have any in his lifetime. But, here he was, amusing a child along with Ashlyn Spencer, the last person he cared to consort with.

It's not that she didn't look pretty...okay, she looked *really* good in her flirty spring-colored dress that whisked to the middle of her long thighs. The curves he'd noticed last week jumped out at him, too, swerving like a race course around her tiny waist, her flat stomach, up to the strain of her modest breasts pushing against her bodice. Her arms were long, graceful as a swan's neck, her legs an endless line of sleek, tanned skin.

Yeah, she was dressed for tug-of-war, all right. A tug from his lust, another from his conscience, warring against each other until he drove himself crazy.

Lighten up, he thought. Where had the old Sam gone? The one who could shout with reckless abandon after a high school football victory? The one who could run a finger over a woman's cheek, enjoying the curve of her smile?

His foster brother, Nick, walked over to him, slapped him on the shoulder. In a gravel-tinged voice, he asked, "Hey, Sam, getting involved in civic duties?"

Sam peered down at his younger brother, still caught in memories, days of football tossing and midnight talks about high school girls. Nick had been escorted out of Kane's Crossing when Chad Spencer had accused him of setting off a bomb in Chaney's Drugstore. When Nick had returned to town, he'd made certain that everyone knew Chad had done the damage. He'd also healed half of the town by releasing them from the Spencers' monetary domination.

Spencers again. Was that all he could think of?

The girl standing next to him, the one with the elfin grin and short, wild hair, was from some pretty evil stock. Even the smooth perfume of her wasn't enough to soften his heart.

Sam quirked a grin at his brother. "Don't get too used to this."

Nick's smile brightened everything around him. Meg had brought out the happiness, and Sam was grateful. The love apparent in their family had attracted him back to Kane's Crossing—a moth drawn to the eternal flame of bad memories. Hopefully, the Cassidys would help him to forget why he'd come running back in the first place.

Nick lowered his voice. "We could always use more people in the Big Brother and Sister program."

"Don't start again."

"Think about it." Nick raised his eyebrows and walked over to Ashlyn, greeting her and Tag with the quiet sort of intensity that was his badge of honor.

A factory employee called Tag's name, and Sam, Ashlyn and the boy lined up against the rope. Sam tried his best to keep his gaze from wandering over Ashlyn's long legs, her smooth derriere.

They'd been matched against a married couple who mentored a husky ten-year-old boy. Sam almost called over to Nick to ask why such a sturdy little bugger had been pitted against Tag, who was basically minus one hand.

But he let it go. As anchor, he'd make up for anything his team required.

Tag took position at the front of their line. He'd received permission to wrap the rope around the wrist of his nubby hand. Sam worried that it might burn him, but he kept his silence, thinking that he just had to live through this for five more minutes, and his work would be done.

Ashlyn firmed her grip on the rope, looking over her shoulder at Sam, scathing his heart with her sweetheart grin. He watched her turn around and dig her Keds tennies into the grass. Sun shined through her thin dress giving him a faint glimpse of more thigh and lacy white panties.

Sam tried to hold it together, feeling that familiar warmth creep into his stomach again.

Hell, maybe she just made him ill. Spencers had that effect on Renos.

The whistle blew, and they tugged with all their might. The other family offered a challenge—especially the bulldog kid in front—but the contest lasted mere seconds.

Before Sam knew it, he was on the ground, a slack rope withered in his palms. Tag had crashed into Ashlyn, and she had conveniently boomed into Sam.

The little boy whooped in victory, joined by Ashlyn's laughter. Sam actually felt a chuckle escape his lungs.

They were a pile of idiots screeching over a meaningless triumph.

Tag sprang to his feet, high-fiving Ashlyn and Sam. Then he ran off to Nick, who supplied another open palm to slap.

Sam could feel Ashlyn's breathing even out, could feel the giggles subside as she realized her position.

He sat up, bringing her with him. She'd landed between his legs, backed against his breath-starved chest, arms draped over his thighs as if he were a damned easy chair. Her flirty little skirt had ridden near the tops of her legs, revealing firm, soft skin as sun-warmed as her sandy hair.

Quickly she pushed the skirt down, causing a thread of disappointment to spin through his body.

"Congratulations, Sheriff Sam. You're quite an anchor."

"No problem." When was she going to get off him? Part of him hoped she wouldn't dare.

"Heavy, stoic, weighed down. The job suits you." She tilted her face over her shoulder to look at him, that cotton-candy smile making his jeans shrink three sizes.

Tag reappeared, holding his good hand out to Ashlyn. ''Wanna do the balloon toss?''

Sam had no idea if she executed her next movements on purpose or with absence of thought—as she'd done that night in his Bronco, before driving up to see her father. That night, she'd scratched her fingers along his arm, making him yearn for the feel of her body pressed to his. Now, she accepted Tag's grasp, her hand trailing along the inside of Sam's leg as she rose upward.

While she walked away, she left Sam sitting in a flustered heap.

And he was a man who rarely got flustered.

Chapter Five

Sam ambled back to his blanket, where Rachel Shane and her six-year-old daughter, Tamela, sucked on Popsicles.

Rachel pinned him down with her sharp, gray-green gaze. "The champion returns."

He shrugged, sat with his knees drawn up, his arms resting on his lower thighs. "Why don't you girls join the fun?"

"I think my best friend has a hold of the situation," Rachel said, referring to Meg. "Besides, I'm not quite sure what fun is anymore."

Tamela wrinkled her nose at him, serious as an owl. "Mom worries that the other kids will break my bones if we all get too excited."

"You're smaller than most children your age, honey." Rachel presented her daughter with the bare Popsicle stick. "Can you throw that away? And I think you can play the egg-toss game without too much of a ruckus.''

Tamela accepted the stick, holding it in front of her as if it were a dead rat, then scooted off to join the other children.

''I'm way too overprotective,'' said Rachel, following her daughter with a wistful gaze.

''You're careful,'' Sam said, knowing exactly why Rachel Shane kept her daughter under such scrutiny.

She shook her head. ''Ever since Matthew left us high and dry, I can't let go of Tamela.''

Sam thought about the stories she'd told during casual family dinners at her horse farm or the Cassidy home. Her husband had disappeared over two years ago, leaving no word or trace of his existence. After quitting her job as an ER nurse and devoting herself to running the farm, Rachel had hired a private detective with very little results. The last they'd heard of Matthew Shane, he'd been in New Orleans. Sam thought a lot of people disappeared there, whether or not they wanted to.

Sam frowned. ''What'll you do if he comes back?''

''I'd make him suffer.'' Rachel let out a throaty laugh. ''I should've known it was coming. Matthew was always a bit restless.''

He didn't know what to say. Rachel had been confiding in him since he'd moved back, updating him on the detective's information and the like. He thought maybe she took comfort from the fact that he was in law enforcement, that he could offer encouragement.

Obviously she was depending on the wrong person for that.

They listened to the laughter of children ringing through the air, each peal like a kick to his gut. He wished he and Mary had raised children, but there hadn't been time. After her death, he'd convinced himself that he wouldn't have been a good father anyway; that he had no more love to give anyone. He'd never opened himself to the possibility since.

His gaze latched on to Ashlyn once again. She was playing the balloon toss with Tag, taking care to aim the water-filled time bomb at the boy's good hand. So far, they were a good team, lasting longer than most of the couples.

He imagined her in the future, married off to some guy rich enough to please her family. He wondered what their kids would look like. Spiked hair? Devils in their colorful eyes?

Sam smiled and, when he caught himself, stopped, hoping Rachel hadn't caught on to his ridiculous musings.

But his blanket companion was too perceptive. She'd have to be with the way she watched her daughter like a hawk. "I can't help noticing your fascination with the town bad girl."

"Who?"

"Please, Sam. She's cute as a button. A bit of the hellion in her, but you can't help admiring spunk like that."

"Buttons aren't cute."

She laughed. "So by-the-book literal. And vigilant. I'll bet you twenty dollars that you can't keep your eyes off her for one minute."

"Why is this an issue?"

He glimpsed at Ashlyn again when Meg went over to say something to her, making them both laugh.

Good thing he hadn't made that bet with Rachel. He hadn't even lasted five seconds without his hungry gaze tracking Kane's Crossing's troublemaker again.

Meg left Ashlyn, and his eyes met hers, fleetingly, enough to tell her that he'd been watching.

A balloon splashed into Ashlyn's shoulder, dousing her with water. She crossed her arms over her chest, sending a saucy grin Sam's way.

Damn, he could imagine the way her dress was probably molded to her breasts, could picture the dusty-pink tips as they pebbled against the air through the thin material.

Suddenly, Meg was by his side, intruding on his forbidden fantasy.

"Rachel, is he still checking out the taboo?"

"Taboo is right," she answered. "Sam can't keep his tongue in his mouth."

The image felt like a bucket of ice-cold water tossed over his head. "Give me the benefit of the doubt."

Meg lightly elbowed Rachel in the ribs. "Yup, always keeping us on our toes, that Ashlyn. Of course, her family hates that she often consorts with us peasants."

"Not that she minds all the trouble," Rachel added. "I think she thrives on it."

Sam couldn't argue with that. He'd seen the sparkle in her eyes up close. "Not that I care, but what does she do with her life? Besides keeping the gossip columns full of ink."

Rachel held out her wrist. A silver bracelet, with intricate designs twisted into a scape of moons and stars, stared back at him. He looked it over, impressed with the detail.

"She did this?" he asked.

Meg nodded. "And more. Nobody really talks about it, but she's a talented sculptor. It's sad though. After she went to the local college, she had the opportunity to study art in Florence, Italy. But she didn't accept the invitation."

Sam furrowed his brow, hating that he was interested enough to ask. "Why?"

"Rumor has it that her mom asked her to stay," Meg said. "Edwina Spencer is always sick, always on her deathbed."

The shadow from the second floor. Sam remembered it from last week. "Ashlyn takes care of her mom?"

Rachel's laugh was pointed. "The best she can. I think the perfect way to encapsulate the Spencer family would be this—warped."

Just as the word finished thudding through his mind, Sam turned back to Ashlyn, who was wrapped in a blanket, talking with the little boy from their tug-of-war.

The crowd parted, and Horatio Spencer filed through the opening, a *Maxim* era, polished young man trailing him. The guy looked fresh out of a fraternity-row ceremony, delivered to the world by the thousands. His slicked hair was snipped to perfection, his skin baked to a tanning-bed glow.

"King Spencer has arrived," whispered Rachel.

Life seemed to fade from the sky; the flying kites

stopped dancing. Horatio stood over his daughter, arms crossed like the gates of his mansion.

Ashlyn sparkled a smile at him and got to her feet, holding out an arm to introduce her little friend Tag. Her father ignored the kid, sending sparks of anger through Sam's chest.

The sparks ignited into a flame as Spencer herded his daughter to the outskirts of the picnic, his younger Wall Street clone in tow.

Rachel sighed. "As I said, warped. What do you bet Horatio Spencer will try to set her up with that stiff-necked junior executive? He's pretty cute, but, come on."

Jealousy. That's what had to be zinging through his limbs. Hot, unwanted and lethal. Ridiculous, too, since he barely even knew her. Didn't *want* to know her, either.

Sam looked away from Ashlyn before he could explode.

He was so ticked off he didn't notice that Tag had plopped onto his blanket. The kid stared at him, a smile etched onto his face.

He thought of the children he'd never have.

Then he willed away the memory. Still, Sam wasn't sure what to do. What did you say to little people? And why did the kid even want to hang around a crusty old lawman like Sam Reno?

Meg's and Rachel's smothered laughter wasn't helping any, either.

The little person was still staring at Sam, at his badge in particular.

He huffed a sigh, removed his weathered lawman's star, made sure the clasp wasn't sticking out to poke any skin and handed it over to Tag.

The child's eyes widened with happiness, his mouth forming an awe-filled "Oh."

There, that'd keep him busy for a few seconds.

In the meantime he turned his attention back to Ashlyn, not liking the fact that his body was ruling his mind.

"Ashlyn, this is Eugene Hampton, of the Vermont Hamptons," said her father, chin tilted up with pride.

"Enchanted," she drawled, clutching the blanket tighter around her body. Underneath she was freezing, vulnerable with her balloon-wet dress leeched to her body.

Eugene clicked together his heels and executed a proper bow.

Yes, he actually clicked his heels, just like Dorothy feverishly wishing she were home and not in this crazy land called Oz.

He spoke. "I've looked forward to meeting you, Ashton."

"Ashlyn," she said, shooting her father a typical I-can't-believe-you-think-this-is-gonna-work glare.

He dismissed her altogether. "Eugene works at a Fortune 500 company. Quite a mind in this young man. Impressive."

Ashlyn scanned Eugene's high cheekbones, his snake-oiled blond hair, his pin-striped business suit in the midst of a spring picnic. Ashlyn almost felt sorry for this guy, sorry for the rejection he was about to earn.

She shifted into sabotage gear, knowing her father expected nothing less of her. "Gee, Eugene, it's been a treat, but I'd like to get back to the fun."

Usually her intended beaus exhibited shock at her forced rudeness, but Eugene was a different breed. He shot a glance to her father, and they both chuckled.

"He's prepared for your difficulties, Ashlyn." Her father nodded at Eugene, then left.

Exasperated, Ashlyn spread out her arms under the blanket, an oh-well gesture.

You ready to take me on? she thought.

Eugene didn't even blink. "How would you like to go for a walk, get away from all this pageantry?"

Not a chance. Ashlyn was done isolating herself. She took in the carnival colors of the picnic with its children running and playing, with its participants starting to creep into the neutral zone to forget the town's divisive past, with its band that had just plugged in and ripped into a popular rock tune.

This was her town. She didn't own it, but she loved it.

Ashlyn positioned herself behind a fluttering banner, the better to keep tabs on her new friend, Tag, and Sam Reno, who sat stiffly on his blanket, looking everywhere but at the child by his side.

She wanted to laugh at his discomfort, this big man who could handle any tough situation, but found it impossible to deal with the brown-eyed moppet who'd befriended them. If the sheriff wasn't careful, he'd have a raging case of hero worship in Tag—if he didn't already.

Eugene's voice droned on. "Ashlyn?"

"Yes?" She avoided making eye contact with her intended, even if he did resemble a manicured, Armani-suited Brad Pitt. "Oh, yeah. You know, I'd really like to stay at the picnic, Eugene."

"I'm on the fast track at Callahan and Dergin."

Ashlyn tore her gaze away from Sam and looked at Eugene in wonder. "Do tell."

That got him started. Ashlyn took the opportunity to return her attention to Tag and Sam.

What kind of father would Sam make? From the way he kept a safe canyon between him and Tag, Ashlyn wasn't sure of the answer. Would he ignore his sons and daughters? Or would his eyes shine with pride at every accomplishment?

Now she was getting fanciful. Sam Reno didn't seem to have a paternal bone in his body. And Ashlyn knew from experience that having an emotionless father was as devastating as not having one at all.

"...and I'll own that place before I'm thirty—"

"Listen," Ashlyn said, slipping into her sweet-as-pie charm mode. "I'm going to be blunt with you, save you some time. Eugene, you're a fine-looking young man, but I've got no interest in dating you, marrying you or bearing your munchkins. I don't know what my father promised, probably lots of money in the future, but it's not going to happen."

Eugene adjusted his tie. "You're direct."

She nodded in agreement. "Yes, I am. And it's not you, understand? I'm sure you'll find a very nice girl. Lots of fish in the sea. All that."

She was anxious to get Sam back in her sights.

Eugene's mouth turned up in a cocky grin. "Your dad said you'd be hard to get."

"All right." Hardball time. "How much money did he offer for you to court me?"

He cleared his throat. "My interest in you has nothing to do with money—"

"You know we were hit hard in the last couple of years. Most of our businesses were bought out."

Eugene didn't seem too surprised. "I thought that wasn't relevant anymore."

Ashlyn raised her brows, allowing her body language to speak for her. She could detect the change sweep over Eugene. From suave suitor to faint disinterest, as if he was wondering if she was worth his valuable time.

He bowed and clicked his heels again. "Charmed, Miss Spencer."

Then he backed off, leaving Ashlyn with a feeling of lightness, however tinged it may have been with anger at her father.

She peeked back at Sam again. Their eyes met.

Then, with the nonchalance of two strangers passing on the street, they looked away from each other.

Three days later Sam filled out paperwork at his office desk, enjoying the sound of an empty room. Although he'd been a low-ranked beat cop in D.C., that and his criminal justice degree had been sufficient enough to get him appointed sheriff of the small county. Now he knew why.

The only problems he'd had to deal with in Kane's Crossing during his short stint as sheriff concerned obnoxious drunks and Ashlyn Spencer. Hardly ulcer inducing.

In D.C., a month with such peace and order wouldn't have existed. As a beat cop, Sam had seen his share of domestic abuse, burglars surprised during their crimes, blood splattered on tenement walls, drug deals gone bad. He'd been jaded enough before visiting his last crime scene—the rubble of an exploded house in the suburbs—that he hadn't needed that extra push into cynicism. It'd been a secret meth lab, destroyed by the cooker—the slime who'd created the methamphetamine—and his bad chemistry.

Sam remembered the feel of crisped grass under his shiny cop shoes as he'd explored the crime scene, the trail of thin blood leading to a child's smoking tennis shoe—

The office door burst open, nudging Sam out of his nightmare. Tag, the boy from the picnic, stood in the doorway, eyes as pathetic as a lost pup's. His silly grin lit the room.

Sam wiped a bead of sweat from his forehead, his voice harsher than normal. "Not again. Your teacher's really going to get you this time."

Tag's smile wavered as his gaze dropped. Guilt overshadowed Sam's soul like clouds shrouding a cold moon.

"Kid, this is the third time in three days you've ditched the center to come here. I don't have time for you to be hanging around." He didn't have time for the useless daydreams, either, the ones in which an anonymous future wife kissed the forehead of a baby, that baby growing up to look just like Tag.

"I'm sorry, sir." Tag peeked up at Sam, devilish grin intact. "But I hate math."

"Well, math does vex me, too. Now scoot back to the center before your teacher has my hide."

Tag still smiled, making Sam wonder what was wrong.

Finally he said, "Mr. Cassidy told me that you want to be my Big Brother."

Damn. He'd told Nick not to say anything because Sam wasn't even sure he wanted to take this plunge. But, ever since the picnic, Nick and Meg had been on his case to "adopt" a Little Brother. So, yesterday, after Tag's second visit, he'd relented, figuring that Tag was always around him anyway.

"It hasn't been finalized, kid." Sam tried to not seem too emotional about the whole thing. He wasn't even sure he'd be a good mentor, wasn't sure he had any love to give to anyone. "Now let me work."

Tag ignored his demand, and he wandered back to the jail cells, which amused Sam a little. The kid reminded him of another hardheaded resident of Kane's Crossing. One Ashlyn Spencer, troublemaker supreme.

He wondered if she'd gone out with that pretty boy from the picnic, if she'd pressed her lips against his.

What would she taste like?

Sam sat up in his chair, scanned his desk for something to do. Being sheriff was supposed to be a busy job. Surely he needed to be doing something other than fantasizing about a woman he didn't even like.

A barren desk. Maybe Deputy Joanson would call on the scanner, requesting help with a jaywalker or something equally as serious.

"Tag, get over here."

The kid scampered to the front of his desk, all but panting with excitement. "Can I wear a star? Can I be a Little Brother deputy?"

"Nope, kid. I've already got one who needs baby-sitting."

"Then why does he get to be deputy?"

Sam grunted. He didn't want to go into all the politics that had discouraged qualified applicants from applying for the deputy position. The former lawmen all had a misplaced fidelity to the dead, Spencer-supported Sheriff Carson. They'd quit the moment they heard Sam Reno was taking over. Gary Joanson, as inexperienced as he was, at least had enthusiasm and loyalty to Sam.

"Listen, Tag. We're going to call the center, and I'm taking you back, all right? No more of this foolishness, loitering around my office. Got it?"

Tag performed a little-kid, I-don't-wanna-go-back shuffle.

Sam shook his head and picked up the phone, having memorized the Reno Center number by now. He spoke to the youth specialist who answered and hung up.

After donning his jacket, he beckoned to Tag, who had taken a seat on the wooden bench near the doorway. Since he needed to drive to Main Street anyway, he might as well drop the kid off at the center on the way. "Come on."

"Oh, boy. Big Brothers take their kids to sports games. Why don't we just do that?"

Probably in reaction to Sam's wry expression, Tag slowly peeled himself away from his seat, making the process a painful one for Sam. How could a child affect him so much? He felt awful, as though he'd failed at this Big Brother thing already.

They drove a block down the road to the center, Tag poking at the vehicle's scanner, searchlight and any other law-related item available. Sam made sure Tag didn't touch the shotgun that rested between them, even if it was locked securely from wandering hands.

Here it was, the Reno Center. Every time Sam saw it, a black wing of sadness shadowed him.

He'd grown up in this one-story home, and his parents had lived here until their dying days. While Nick had been buying up property in town, he'd purchased this structure, as well, renovating it to house about fifty wards of the court—children without parents.

It didn't much resemble the home of his youth anymore. Nick had added more rooms to the original building as well as cottages that acted as dormitories for the children. He'd even constructed athletic fields on the ample acreage so the kids could run through the grass until their legs cried for them to stop.

Additionally, Nick had brought in a woman from Michigan, an expert who'd run a similar center there. She'd hired a licensed clinical social worker to act as a counselor, a psychiatrist, private tutors to provide education, youth specialists and an on-call nurse. Rachel Shane, an ex-ER nurse, had decided to volunteer time for the last job, and Meg Cassidy, of course, ran the Big Brother and Sister program.

Sam helped Tag out of the Bronco, handling the boy as if he were a sack of groceries. Damn, he'd never get the swing of having someone so young around.

The kid peered up at him, curly dark hair sorely in need of a cut. Sam wondered if they'd let him take Tag to town to get one.

"Suppose I'll have to do a time-out, Sheriff Reno?"

"At least."

They walked in the front door and, for a minute, Sam thought he could smell mom's pumpkin pie cooling in the converted kitchen.

The receptionist smiled at him. If Sam didn't know any better, he'd say most women in Kane's Crossing were just plain man hungry. "Hello, Sheriff. Thank you for taking care of this one."

She frowned at Tag, who responded by grinning.

"Where should I take him?" Sam asked, bristling at the way she was scolding the kid without saying a damned word. Nobody would talk to his Little Brother that way, right?

"Let's see." She consulted a computer screen. "He's now scheduled to be in the literacy lab."

She gave him directions while Tag wandered ahead of him. Sam took to his heels and followed the kid, passing the library, which housed books, computers and tutoring rooms, the woodwork-lined dining room and kitchen, which had its own full-time staff, and the cozy common room, where children gathered to socialize and watch television. Plump sofas and warm colors invited the children to relax, to feel good about being here.

Sam couldn't believe how much Nick and Meg had spent on the Reno Center, but he was damned proud of them. His own parents had taken in Nick when he was a young rebel, and their hearts had broken when he'd been falsely accused of bombing Chaney's Drugstore. Had they been alive to witness Nick's return to Kane's Crossing, they would've been ecstatic.

But they wouldn't have taken any of Nick's money, no matter how rich his little brother was. He'd amassed a fortune by purchasing businesses and reselling them, by diverting the profits to sound investments. Nick was magnanimous to a fault, having used ample funds to help Kane's Crossing's poorer population.

And his generosity extended to Sam, as well. However, when Nick had suggested that *he* buy Sam's new house for him, Sam's hackles had risen.

"I've got enough money to share with all my family," Nick had said.

Sam had refused him, politely but firmly, without leaving an opening for another offer. Nick hadn't brought it up since.

Tag turned a corner and disappeared into the literacy lab with its plethora of computers, games and books. His teacher looked up from the story she was reading to the class to give Tag a stern look before continuing.

Sam reluctantly backed out of the room. That kid was surely in for it.

On his way out of the center, Sam heard giggling in a curtained alcove, so he paused, then peeked into its shadowed privacy.

Nick and Meg nuzzled each other like two teenagers. Meg blushed, and Nick cleared his throat as they stepped into the hallway.

"Sorry, big brother," Nick said, grinning at Meg.

"It was just one tiny kiss." Meg whispered so only Sam could hear. "We're actually very careful around the children."

Sam merely held up his hands—*don't involve me*—and stepped into the reception area.

With a start, he saw Ashlyn Spencer grinning up at him.

"Hi, Sheriff," she said, cutting him with her bright stained-glass eyes. "Trouble in this paradise?"

Sam felt his eyebrow cock in consternation.

Nick said, "Ashlyn, Sam's not playing sheriff right now. He's our newest Big Brother."

Meg turned to Sam, making him flush with embarrassment. "And we're forever grateful."

Then she put her hand on Nick's arm. "That's great news for Tag, getting a Big Brother and Big Sister in the same week."

Sam and Ashlyn traded a look, territorial tension marking the atmosphere.

His voice scratched as he said, "You're telling me that Miss Spencer is Tag's Big Sister?"

"I was getting around to it," Meg said.

Ashlyn stood up, and Sam couldn't help noticing the way her breasts were outlined by her lacy top, the way her colorful jeans hugged her long legs. "It's okay, Meg. Maybe Sam will mentor another child."

He stepped forward. "Tag already knows that I've accepted."

"Same deal." She faced him, arms crossed over her chest. "As a matter of fact, I came here to spend time with him today."

Meg moved over to put her arm around Ashlyn. "It's okay, you two. We do have other people who barely knew each other when they accepted the Big Sibling position. There haven't been any problems so far."

Nick looked at his wife with suspicion. "*So far.* Can I talk to you?"

Husband and wife disappeared into the next room, urgent whispers dominating their conversation.

Ashlyn sighed and put her hands on her hips. "So are we going to break this kid's heart?"

She stared at him, waiting for an answer.

Chapter Six

Ashlyn felt six shades of angry-red as Sam frowned at her.

What gave him the upper hand here, anyway? Did he own Tag?

As soon as she realized how petty she sounded, even to herself, Ashlyn's temper cooled. Why was she so stuck on Taggert? Especially since there were other orphaned children at the Reno Center who probably needed a Big Sister?

The answer was obvious. Tag had touched her heart, even in the short time she'd known him. Besides, yesterday, when she'd stopped by the Reno Center to drop off some art supplies for all the children, she'd seen him sitting by himself in the common room, alone, watching a rerun of ''The Brady Bunch.'' The sitcom had enthralled Tag as Ashlyn had watched him from the doorway and, as soon as the child had seen her standing there, he'd raced from the chair to slap her a high-five leftover from their picnic victories.

At that moment the earth had shaken, the angels had sung. She'd thought, Little old me can make a difference in someone's life.

Then, when Tag had asked her to be his Big Sister, Ashlyn had accepted with no reservations whatsoever. She'd settled the matter with Meg, who hadn't mentioned Sam's involvement.

Sneaky Meg. But how could Ashlyn blame her when she was just doing what was best for Tag?

Sam gestured to a couch in the reception area. Ashlyn noticed that the cute assistant at the desk kept shooting appreciative glances his way.

"Let's figure this out ourselves," he said.

He took a seat on one end of the upholstered love seat, she took the other end in response. Obviously he wanted to be as far away from her as possible. She felt as if the line that'd been drawn at the picnic, separating the two of them, existed even now.

"It's an easy call, Sheriff Sam."

"Sam. You make me sound like I'm on 'The Howdy Doody Show.'"

She laughed. He didn't.

"Anyway," she continued, "we can both mentor Tag. It doesn't mean we need to bond with each other, just the child."

"So no family photos at the Mercantile at Christmas. Nothing like that?"

Was she that repulsive to him? "That depends on Tag."

Sam nodded, and she could see the wheels turning

in his mind. A million ways to leave Ashlyn Spencer in the dust.

"I think we can both handle this with a certain degree of maturity," he said.

"We'll just treat each other as acquaintances. I promise, I won't contaminate you with my Spencerness."

Sam's heavy gaze bored into her. "Let's not make that an issue."

"Okay, moratorium on all the family tension. But we really need to make sure that we're not acting like a divorced couple with visitation rights."

"Right."

Her eyes traveled to his badge. The rust seemed as crusty as his personality. "Right."

Meg entered the room, a smile hiding under a humbled expression. "Pardon the interruption. Is everything okay?"

Sam looked at her; she looked at him. They both managed a yes.

"Wonderful." Meg started to leave, but Nick had walked into the room and stood behind her, watching the events from beneath a lowered brow.

"Everything's fine," Meg said.

Nick turned her back around. "You were saying?"

Meg heaved a sigh. "I apologize for this inconvenience. I thought Tag would be better off with the two of you. After all, you were a great team during tug-of-war."

Ashlyn remembered leaning back against the strength of Sam's chest when they'd fallen. Hearing his heartbeat. Feeling the corded comfort of his arms.

Yeah, they were quite a team. Too bad he didn't know it.

Meg sat between them, taking both their hands. "Tag needs you two. A halfway house for children brought him here two weeks ago, scared, lonely, but still smiling through it all. I have no idea what he's been through. He won't even talk with the counselor. Some of the kids think he was living on the streets in Cincinnati."

Ashlyn peered at the carpet, thinking of her family's rambling mansion and how many homeless people could be sheltered by its bounty. She noticed the lines around Sam's mouth hardening, as well.

What kind of memories were shaping his thoughts about Tag?

Meg continued. "All I'm saying is that Tag lights up when he's around you two. I thought I'd have to tie him to the ground at the picnic last weekend because he was going to take off like a balloon. He's special."

Ashlyn clasped Meg's hand in both of hers. "I can do it."

Sam shifted in his seat, but Ashlyn could tell he'd been affected. His gaze had gotten a little softer, his frown a little more resigned. This flash of emotion tugged at her heart, made her realize that, maybe, Sam wasn't stone-cold, after all.

"Meg, you should've been a used-car salesman," he said.

She said, "I'm not trying to talk you into anything. If either one of you has any doubts about mentoring Tag, say something now or forever hold your peace."

A thick pause made the lobby feel like a sauna.

Ashlyn wasn't about to abandon Tag, and she hoped, for the boy's sake, Sam wouldn't, either.

In fact, working with Sam Reno sounded like pure heaven to her.

Meg must've recognized Sam's reticence. "Sam, are you willing to forget any difficulties you're having with Ashlyn?"

Heck, it sounded like they were being scolded on an elementary-school playground. "Meg," Ashlyn said, "it won't be a problem. Right, Sam?"

He nodded. "Right."

Meg stood, brushing her hands together in a show of relief. "Thanks, you two. He's never going to forget this."

Then she left, looking over her shoulder, probably to see that they weren't going to tear each other to shreds once she vacated the room.

Ashlyn followed suit, more anxious than ever to visit with Tag. "So. Looks like we've got our work cut out for us, huh, Sam?"

But he didn't seem to be listening.

His gaze began at her loopy sandals, traveled up her pants, waist, chest, throat… A physical sensation warming her, teasing her.

A rusty, slanted grin was her answer. "Looks that way."

She left in a hurry, and, once out of sight, leaned against the wall to fan herself.

"Whoo," she mumbled. "I do believe I'm on fire."

And she burned for him the rest of the day.

For two days Sam mulled over Ashlyn's sweet perfume. He thought about how she probably rubbed almond-and-honey lotion into her skin every morning, how she dabbed the scent behind her ears and knees, at the pulse of her wrist.

Forget it, he told himself for the millionth time.

Sam leaned against the hood of the Bronco, having parked it along Main Street to check out the pattern of life in Kane's Crossing. Reactions from the townsfolk differed from chipper greetings to outright hostility in the stares of those who supported the Spencers.

He was damned sick of the whole war already, and he'd lived here for only two months.

Deputy Joanson had told him a rumor that Horatio Spencer was planning to start a new grocery store in town, one to rival the market Nick had purchased and bequeathed to a poorer family. If that was true, tensions would get uglier. He'd have to keep his eye out for trouble.

He scanned Main Street, the Mercantile Department Store with its early summer-fun displays in the front windows, the tiny children's bookstore, Meg's busy-as-a-beehive bakery.

Sam narrowed his gaze. Was that Ashlyn and Tag, down by the barbershop?

They went inside, and Sam's stomach tightened. Hey, hadn't it been his idea to get Tag's haircut?

Granted, he and the boy had already broken the Big Brother ice by shooting some hoops yesterday at the center, and he knew Ashlyn had finger-painted with him and some of the other kids last night, but getting hair chopped off was a man's territory. Ashlyn would probably direct the barber to do something foofy to the kid's scalp.

Sam ambled down Main Street, barely noticing a

group of youngsters who scrambled out of his path when he passed. One of them muttered, "Daggone, he looks ticked."

Lighten up, Sam, he thought once more.

He came up to the shop, pushing open the glass door with the faded red-and-white candy-cane pole out front. The aroma of lime shaving cream and Vitalis hair tonic hovered over the shop, but far be it from him to stop and smell the beauty products.

There they were, near the back of the store, barely visible through the adjustable chairs and old men who'd stopped here to gossip. The ramble of a television game show doused the room with noise.

"Sheriff Reno," a seated barber said with great reverence, lowering his paper as Sam passed.

The other men grunted a greeting, obviously wary of the new sheriff and his presence in the shop.

A second barber stood over Tag, scissors poised for damage. Ashlyn sat in a nearby chair, the remaining barber ready to cut her fairy-clipped mane.

"Look who's here, Tag," she said.

The kid all but jumped out of the chair to welcome him. Sam held out a hand, shaking Tag's. The little guy pumped it with vigor.

Ashlyn's tight voice hadn't fooled Sam. Hell, she was probably as ecstatic to see him as he was her.

"Taggert's getting a cut?" he asked.

Sam knew her grin held back a perky retort. But they'd promised Meg that they'd keep their personal problems away from the Big Brothering. And he intended to keep that vow, just as Ashlyn had.

Tag spoke up as the kid's barber watched Sam, no doubt wondering whether or not to begin.

"We're all doing an activity together," Tag said,

noting something so obvious that it'd slipped Sam's attention.

He guessed he could stand being in Ashlyn's company as long as Tag was happy. So he took the hint and tried not to grumble to himself as he sat in the next empty chair. The barber who'd been reading the *Kane's Crossing Gazette* hefted himself out of his seat and armed himself with clippers.

Sam instructed the fellow to trim his already-short hair, thinking, What the hell? He liked to keep his style orderly, regimented.

While the clippers buzzed near his ear, the two other barbers started on Ashlyn and Tag. Sam spied on his mentoring partner in the mirror.

With a *zist* of the scissors, a hank of hair landed on the clean, white sheet covering Ashlyn's body, and her mouth twisted in a wistful curve. He tried to remember what she'd looked like when she'd worn it as long as Rachel Shane's.

Admit it, he thought. She'd still be delicate-featured and beautiful, even with a crew cut.

He caught her eye as she peeked up, a blush suffusing her cheeks. Somehow the surreal mirror image made him feel as if conversation could be safe, distanced.

"I didn't realize you needed a haircut," he said.

She slid a gaze over to Tag, who chuckled.

"I talked Miss Spencer into it, sir. Haircuts are no fun by yourself."

Ashlyn laughed and "Oo-ohed," the two sounds mixing to form a hybrid of gaiety and caution. "Hey, Harvey, not so short, all right?"

Sam felt himself getting all soft inside, like a jelly doughnut, oozing too much emotion. He trained his gaze on everyone else in the shop, avoiding Ashlyn and her quick smile.

Beneath walls plastered with product advertisements and Spencer High football pictures, the gossipy old men watched Sam, Ashlyn and Tag. Obvious curiosity had halted their conversation.

Were they wondering if the earth was heading toward its final days? If it was snowing in hell? After all, it wasn't every day you saw a Reno and Spencer getting along, entertaining a kid, to boot.

Sam tried to avoid their inspection, his gaze roving the walls instead. Lots of Chad Spencer hero pictures, not that Sam minded. He'd played on the same Varsity football team with Chad for a year, a linebacker to Spencer's quarterback. They hadn't been friends and they hadn't been enemies; those had been the days before the trouble. Before his father had died, before they'd known about Chad's lie regarding Nick and the Chaney Drugstore bombing.

A small picture graced the corner of the barbershop. If Sam squinted, he could see himself, dressed in full uniform, posing for his only newspaper picture.

He almost smiled at the innocence of it: his too-long, hot-rod hair, his relaxed grip on the football helmet's facemask. That's all that had mattered then—sports, girls, cars and family.

And some things never changed.

Ashlyn popped out of her chair, the barber whipping off her towel as if ushering a skittish bull into an arena.

"Have any gel?" she asked.

The stone-faced man rubbed some gooey stuff over his hands and ran it through her short hair, giving it some body. Sam almost envied the guy, fingering hair that looked so soft it moved like silk scarves on a breeze.

Ashlyn picked up a dryer, subjected her hair to it briefly, then jabbed at her head. Voilà, back to normal, wild as a windy day.

He cleared his throat, making himself indifferent to her exuberance, her color and light.

She came to linger near his chair, leaning over the front of him to investigate the barber's technique. "What do you think, Tag? Does the cut make him seem leaner and meaner than usual?"

Tag's barber whisked a minibroom over the kid's shoulders. Most of his curls had been cut off, but he looked pretty respectable. "Sheriff always comes off as mean."

Sam adapted his driest tone of voice. "I'd take mean any day over looking like a Q-Tip."

Tag giggled, and Sam's barber removed his sheet. Ashlyn left her perch to stand behind him.

"I've got this," he heard her say.

She took the broom from the man, who didn't seem at all taken aback by her behavior. Probably most people in Kane's Crossing expected the unexpected from Ashlyn Spencer.

But Sam wasn't quite ready for the whisper-light, jabby drag of the straw over his shoulders, over his neck. She worked the broom with care, and Sam couldn't help feeling helium-headed, turned-on.

He couldn't say a word because the speech stuck in his mouth like peanut butter. Shutting up was a viable option at this point.

Instead, he tried to relax, tried to not think of how he'd sat at home by himself night after night, his muscles aching for someone to rub the tension away. He'd never allowed anyone to creep that close to him. Not for years. And he couldn't do it now.

Sam grabbed Ashlyn's wrist, implying that she needed to stop.

She did, hesitating, then jolted her hand away from his touch, turning her attention to Tag. "I see some stray hairs on you, too, Mr. Taggert."

As she brushed the child's flannel shirt, Sam noticed that she bit her lip, and her skin had pinked.

She had no business touching him like that. He couldn't allow anyone to ever sneak into his life, his heart, again. Losing another woman would slash more wounds into his soul. He couldn't take the pain of the inevitable loss—not again.

Ashlyn finished her work and, over her quiet protests, Sam paid the barbers. She thanked him, avoiding his gaze.

He'd bruised her feelings—that was obvious. But bruises were far less agonizing than what he'd go through if he let another woman touch him like that.

As they stepped onto Main Street, a brisk spring breeze fluttered over his neck, reminding him of Ashlyn's touch. He shut his mind to the rush of life that threatened to overwhelm him.

Ashlyn took Tag's hand. "Good seeing you, Sheriff Reno."

"Yeah," Tag said, "thanks for the haircuts."

Sam shoved his hands into his jeans' pockets, his fingers sliding over something he'd brought just for Tag.

"Before I forget," he said, dragging out his simple gift, "this is for you."

Sam handed the object to the kid. His eyes lit up. "Wow, sir. Thank you!"

He held up a toy badge, the plastic gleaming brighter than even Sam's star did. Sam helped Tag pin it to his shirt, and the kid stuck out his bony chest, his stern expression reflecting pride.

"Now I'm your deputy," Tag said.

Sam cocked a brow, lowered his chin sheepishly. "We'll talk about that later when I stop by."

"Shoot some hoops again?"

"Yeah."

Sam could feel Ashlyn's gaze, how it weighed on him like ten tons of responsibility. When he looked up, she grinned at him—not with the smile of someone thinking up trouble, but with a disconcerting measure of approval.

"Miss Spencer." He nodded at her, then at Tag.

And as he walked away, he couldn't, for the life of him, extinguish his hard-won grin, couldn't forget how good her endorsement felt.

Realization slapped him hard, stunning him. Did he want to avoid Ashlyn because of her family? Or was it because of something more painful, something he'd promised never to put himself through again after Mary died?

It took very little effort for Sam to clear his mind, to fade into the crowd, to become a ghost once again.

Chapter Seven

Two days later Ashlyn, her father and Tag stood in front of the wall that encircled the Spencer estate. Twilight deepened the darkness of her father's eyes, the color-drip melange of the finger-painted bricks a study in contrast.

Ashlyn could feel the anger ebbing upward, forcing words out of her mouth. ''I can't believe you're fuming over something so easily fixed. You only just drove up in your car. You've no idea what happened here.''

Ashlyn turned toward Tag. Tears trembled on his long lashes, and Sam's plastic star shone on his chest, making her all the more sorry for him. It hadn't been Tag's fault that she'd left him alone to get sodas from the main house. It hadn't been his fault that he'd finger-painted over the front of the stately wall ensconcing their mansion. An eight-year-old wouldn't realize that there was a huge difference between the Reno Center's older kids painting murals on the common room walls and Tag splashing pictures on Spencer property.

And, to think, she'd brought him to her home so they could enjoy the clear skies, so they could do some artwork under the shade of a drooping willow in front of the gate. She'd never anticipated this disaster.

Horatio all but sneered at Tag. "I've called up the sheriff, and I intend to see that something is done about this." He indicated the wall. "Look at this…this horrifying vandalism."

Ashlyn put a hand on Tag's shoulder. "You never were a patron of the arts, Father."

Just as Horatio swelled up to answer, Sam Reno's Bronco roared over to the closed gate. He parked it next to Horatio's abandoned Mercedes and exited the vehicle, ambling over to their tense group, hands coming to rest on his utility belt. The intensity of his scowl increased his bulk tenfold, making Ashlyn shrink away in abject shame.

She wondered how he and her father would handle coming face-to-face—Reno to Spencer. Ashlyn was almost happy that she was the focal point of trouble, as usual; it might divert their attention from the deeper issues at hand.

Sam stood silent.

What now? he'd be thinking. She'd seem stupid in his eyes, a spoiled girl who made more trouble for him. An immature brat.

She checked on Tag, seeing how he was holding up under all this thunderous silence, this lack of communication.

Her throat closed up. Tag was trying to smile at Sam through his tears, as if he wasn't facing some mean trouble from Horatio Spencer, one of the town's most powerful men.

What she'd do for this kid.

Sam exchanged a terse glance with Horatio, then speared a look at the wall, his gruff features hardly registering surprise. His gaze traveled to Tag, to her.

A vein in her neck fluttered. He sure wasn't happy about being here.

He said, "I suppose this is the problem?"

Horatio folded his Dior-suited arms across his chest. "One of those Reno Center kids. I knew when they opened it a couple months ago that it'd be trouble. Sheriff, I want this dealt with."

Those Reno Center kids. She could almost feel Sam's hackles rise.

"We'll see what gets dealt with."

Both men bristled at Sam's growl.

Horatio didn't like the town help talking back to him. Ashlyn knew this from years of observation. And Sam evidently hadn't taken too kindly to her father's assumption that he'd be a Spencer puppet, willing to obey commands at the snap of a thumb and a finger.

She could bet that on an even deeper level, they were both thinking of Sam's father. His death. The hard feelings surrounding it.

Ashlyn couldn't stand it anymore. She hated to encourage lying but, for Tag's sake and for the purpose of saying something—*anything*—to break the tension, she had to do it.

Especially when the punishment her father wanted for the orphan scared her to death. He probably wouldn't blink at sending Tag out of the county, out of their oh-so-pleasant lives.

Her mind whirred with anxiety. "Sheriff, no matter what my father says, I was the one who treated the town to another artistic display—this time on my family's wall, for all the world to see."

Her father looked about ready to strangle her. "Dammit, Ashlyn."

Sam's expression revealed that he wasn't impressed with her story. She wondered if he would get Tag into trouble by questioning the veracity of her claim.

She glared at him, willing him to keep quiet, to accept her lie.

Sam locked gazes with her. She held the weight of it, stomach quivering with hope. Hope that he'd believe this lie. Hope that he'd see her as more than a Spencer, as more than a young girl who'd longed for his kiss one night under an October moon.

After an endless moment a slight grin slanted over his mouth. *You win…for now,* it said.

He turned to Tag. "Is that the truth? Miss Spencer painted the wall?"

Was it just her, or did his tone hold a measure of disbelief?

She forced her glare away from Sam, to Tag. Don't blow it, she thought.

The little boy's voice trembled. "I—"

Pause. He was about to incriminate himself so she wouldn't get into trouble; she could feel it in the hesitation.

There was no way Tag would understand the dynamics of this situation. If Ashlyn confessed, it'd make her father big-time mad, that was for sure. But she didn't mind. The wall-painting adventure would merely be another thing they didn't talk about, another thing that would fester between them. Like the way he loved Chad more than he did her.

Like the time in the cave…

Ashlyn swallowed, trying to forget the darkness, the loneliness. "Why are you putting Taggert under this sort of pressure, Sheriff? This sort of mischief is all over my file at your office. *I did it.*"

The soft comfort of slightly misshapen fingers warmed her heart as Tag slid his hand into her fist.

He obeyed her. He never said a word.

At that moment Ashlyn couldn't imagine life without this kid, couldn't imagine going back to her irreverent jokester disguise, her mule-headed attempts to hide her vulnerable side from the world. Her energy would be much better spent like this, holding Tag's hand, helping him walk through life.

Sam must have recognized her determination to protect Tag. Maybe there was even a glimmer of admiration in his otherwise flat eyes as he faced Horatio.

"How do you want your daughter dealt with?"

Ashlyn almost chided Sam for the statement's mocking undertone. She wondered if this was some sort of victory for the Renos, if Sam was, even now, wallowing in secret celebration at Horatio's reaction.

Her father had turned to her, the proud set of his shoulders slumped, a deflated question in his gaze.

Why does it have to be like this?

But as soon as she identified his feelings, they were erased by a haughty lift of his brows. "We'll talk about this later, Ashlyn."

He addressed Sam. "And you... Just because the county hired you doesn't mean I enjoy having a poverty-rat Reno on my property."

Ashlyn sucked in a breath, ready to spirit Tag away from the scene if the unavoidable confrontation between these two men exploded. Already, she could see Sam holding himself back, straightening his stance.

What could she say to dispel the tension? Should she resort to pulling another prank, lightening the harsh atmosphere? She'd done this flippant trouble-shooting her whole life, soothing tempers and reputations until her own standing in the community had amounted to nothing more than a joke itself.

While she searched for an answer, the air vibrated with ill feelings, years of unspoken hate circling their heads.

Sam opened his mouth, his lips hard as an insult. Then he looked at Ashlyn, at Tag. He sealed off his words, staring at the painted wall.

Ashlyn's father seemed satisfied with the silence, probably thinking he'd gotten the better of Sam. He straightened his tie, turned on his heel and slid into the fine-leather comfort of his Mercedes. The front gates glided open, and he was gone.

As the gates shut again, leaving out the rest of the world, Ashlyn thought, *I wish we'd talk about this later.*

Yet she knew they wouldn't. They never did.

She hid her face from Sam, hoping he wouldn't discover the regret she harbored. Teary heat covered her eyes, making a blur of the green grass, of the cocoa-smoothness of Tag's hand clasped in hers.

"Miss Spencer," Tag said, "I just wanted to show you my picture."

She cleared her throat, aware that Sam was probably watching. She didn't want to see his face—the hurt, the disappointment, the anger for her father. "I know, I know. I shouldn't have even brought you over—"

"I'm sorry," he said.

"I don't mind, Tag." And she didn't. She wanted to keep him out of a worse situation than he was in now, with being an orphan, with having to live in a cottage full of kids in the same hopeless boat.

It didn't seem fair.

Sam's voice interrupted her thoughts. "Tag, why don't you hop in the car and wait for me?"

Tag hugged her, and Ashlyn responded. He didn't need to say thank you, didn't even need to tell her he'd never do it again. The contact was enough promise.

He skittered away, the car door's metallic bang signaling his absence.

Ashlyn took a deep breath and gathered herself to look Sam in the eye. What she saw wasn't the hatred she expected. Instead, where a slant of late light filtered through the willow leaves, she detected a resolute sadness, compassion etched in the lines of his face.

She got the feeling that he was more concerned about the way her father had brushed her off. Sam's attention shamed her because she really wasn't *that* kind of person, deserving of pity. The kind who gave selflessly to others.

On the other side of the painted brick wall, sprinklers came to life, hissing, watering the expansive lawn. The sound resembled whispers, accusations.

In spite of everything, this situation was serious.

She'd involved Tag in a lie and, while it'd saved his hide from Horatio Spencer, it didn't sit well with her.

And she knew that Sam knew.

Ashlyn couldn't wait any longer. "I'm sorry about that."

"They were just words, that's all. I'm more worried about..." He trailed off.

Sam stepped closer, reached out, ran his fingers over her hair. Something as nebulous as a memory clouded his eyes as Ashlyn almost reared back from his touch, from the sear of heat. Her heart thudded from the unexpected gesture, but at the same time, she knew why he was showing such compassion.

Her father's callousness had probably made him feel sorry for her, and she couldn't stand the thought of it.

She tried to recapture her breath. "No lectures, please. You know I can't stand words of wisdom. It's entirely against my nature to follow common sense."

If a tear hadn't chosen that moment to meander out of her eye, she might have pulled off the tough act. Embarrassed by her inability to act as if her father's frosty attitude didn't matter, Ashlyn looked away from Sam.

He tipped her chin with a finger, moving her gaze back to his. A live wire seemed to connect them, sizzling, pulling him closer...close enough so that Ashlyn felt his breath heat over her lips. She closed her eyes, basking under the warmth, the gentle touch of his fingertips.

He pressed against her, the pressure of his mouth intensifying, fitting against her own lips like rainwater sluicing over skin—moist and sleek-soft.

Her body whirled with emotion, tying her feelings in a red flower-ribbon knot.

Did this mean Sam Reno cared for her? Even if his kiss was just a sign of pity? Or maybe it was a method of getting back at Horatio, taking whatever was his.

He ran a finger over her shoulder blade, making her shiver, then traced his lower lip over hers with pulse-stretching care.

His mouth was as soft as she'd always imagined—light as a fall of rose petals, warm as a summer nap in a meadow. He felt so right next to her, their scents mingling to form a perfume like no other.

She felt herself balancing on the edge of a needful sob, caught between the urge to push away from him and the compulsion to nestle closer. Kisses so perfect should have the power to last forever, and she willed the contact to fly, to span the distance between his existence and hers.

But it ended all too soon, just as quickly as it had started. Sam stepped back as if he'd cut himself with a hot shard of stained-glass. His eyes gave off an intense heat, revealing a hunger that reached far beyond his gruff exterior.

Ashlyn's heart jolted with the possibility that he wanted her. That much was clear from his feral burn, his jagged breathing.

She watched him change in front of her, jaw muscles flexing, hands clenching, grabbing thin air. In moments he was back—the Sam Reno she knew. The man with the desolate hazel eyes.

It was as if it'd never happened. Sam resumed his lawman's stance, his cool, judgment-day detachment. He avoided her gaze as if she was a mistake he wanted to forget.

Ashlyn tried to laugh off the awkward moment, slough off the all-consuming buzz of his after touch. "Hey, just make sure Tag has some fun tonight. He's a trouper."

Sam took a couple more steps back, as if to put a wall between the two of them. The space he left felt cold, hard as bricks.

He cleared his throat. Back to business. "I'd say he's not the only trouper here. Will you be in trouble?"

Her lips still burned from his kiss, her skin tingled with the electricity of his touch. She couldn't believe he was ignoring what had just happened. Ignoring things just like her family did.

"Why would I be in more trouble?" she asked, hating that she was practicing a little avoidance herself. They'd just *kissed,* for heaven's sake, and both of them were too proud to drag any emotional baggage into the open.

"Stop pretending, Ashlyn. We both know the story here."

Hope made her perk up, but his serious gaze made her realize that he wasn't talking about the kiss at all.

"You don't know anything, Sam." She pointed to a dark blue splash on the wall. "See? This represents dictatorship and the pain it causes. It's a statement.''

He held up his hands, backed away some more. ''Have it your way.''

''And you know that I love trouble. I guess I do have some more waiting for me once I cross these gates.'' There. Flippancy should convince him, should relieve this tension.

Sam's voice seemed huskier than usual, an undertone of gravity beneath the wry tenor. ''So you will have a hard time with your dad?''

What would he think about her father setting her up with every Eugene Hampton in the world? ''It's nothing much. It's just...'' A burn of heat surrounded the patch of skin where his hand had been. Heck, her lips could barely form words, they were so hot.

But what did she have to lose by spilling her deep, dark secrets? ''My father's angry this time because I told a would-be boyfriend that we're not as rich as Father likes everyone to believe. Having said that, however, I'd appreciate it if you wouldn't spread the word.'' She grinned. ''We still have some family pride, you know.''

No response.

All right, so it'd been thoughtless of her to reveal something so personal about the Spencers. But why shouldn't everyone, including Sam Reno, know?

Time to fill the silence with more prattle. His reticence tended to do that to a girl. ''Don't be angry with me. I'm learning how to take care of Tag, Sam. Cut me some slack.''

He slanted her a faint grin, and she couldn't help

returning the gesture. She'd tasted that full lower lip, and now, she wanted more.

She stepped around the Bronco to wave goodbye to Tag. He turned to the window and rolled it down.

"By the way, Sheriff," she said softly. "I love your deputy's badge."

Sam's neck grew ruddy, but he remained silent. She knew she'd hit the red circle in the middle of the mortification target, but that was beside the point. He'd made Tag's chest swell with pride, with importance. A man who'd do that for a child was something to treasure. To dream about.

"Sir?" Tag asked. "You promised we'd go fishing tomorrow."

Fishing? Ashlyn tried to seem wounded at being left out of the fun.

Tag continued. "Can Miss Spencer go?"

Ashlyn could almost hear Sam's mind screaming for a way out of this one. She could let him off the proverbial hook, she supposed, bow out of the situation. Or she could make him squirm.

Squirming wouldn't do any harm. "Fishing? Sounds like a good time."

Sam peered at the darkening skyline, avoiding her altogether. "Can you drag yourself out of bed at four in the morning?"

Her inner alarm clock wailed with grief. "Sure can."

As Sam stared at her in doubt, Ashlyn puffed up with determination.

He sighed. "We'll pick you up then."

Tag did a victory dance in his seat, and Sam never looked more uncomfortable.

After she slept a lonely sleep in the silence of her

family's mansion tonight, Ashlyn was going to spend a day touching squishy things with Sam Reno. Sounded like Shangri-la to her.

As the 4:30 a.m. sun peeked over the tree-lined horizon at Cutter's Lake, Sam tried once again to explain hook baiting to Ashlyn, who seemed as perky as ever—even at daybreak. Splinters from the dock poked at the seat of his pants, exacerbating Sam's crusty mood.

He'd gone from crazy to growly in the space of a day. And it'd all started with that damned—albeit hot—kiss he'd planted on Ashlyn last night. Well, truth be told, his foul mood had developed even earlier, when she'd refused to tell the truth about Tag's finger painting. It had then escalated with Horatio's sharp words. Oddly enough, the barb hadn't bothered him as much as he'd expected. The fact that Ashlyn had involved Tag in an outright lie—no matter how much trouble it saved Tag—bothered him more.

Tag had told the whole story: about how she'd gone inside to get him a root beer, about how he'd seen the big kids painting on walls at the center and thought it'd be okay for him to do it, too, about how he thought Ashlyn would enjoy his art on such a large canvas…

So the boy knew that what he'd done was wrong. Sam had made sure of it.

Ashlyn was another case all together.

She wrinkled her nose, looking like a sparkly-eyed elf who'd crept out of the woods to make some trouble. A female version of Puck, with her short hair tufted and dawn-burnished.

"Sam, couldn't you just bait it?" She grinned up at him.

His heart took a flying leap into oblivion, remembering how he'd kissed those lips last night. He did his best to grab his emotions back, to ignore the sensation of losing all control. "Hey, I'm an equal-opportunity fisherman. All of us have to pull our weight."

Tag stood next to him on the dock, his fishing line pooling like a webby squiggle on the water's smooth surface. He reeled in his bait. "You did it for me."

Sam couldn't count on the kid for support. "The first time. You're next, buddy."

"Can't I just use a plastic worm?" Ashlyn asked. "I don't like the thought of that poor live one wrenching around in agony."

He'd never take a woman fishing again. Hell, he hadn't even taken his wife when she was alive. Her tastes had run more to the sedate: listening to big band music at the local bar, watching their favorite programs on TV, reading a good book before bedtime. Normal stuff.

Sam smiled wryly. "That's what you do when you're fishing, sweetheart. There's some suffering involved."

"Humph." She leaned over to the tackle box and extricated a plastic, purple worm. With ease, she secured it on the hook and cast a graceful fishing line arc into the lake.

Sam shook his head and returned to the contemplation of his own dead line. Yeah, fishing. A time for thought, a time for reflection.

It was killing him. Every time he was reduced to

thinking, Ashlyn's sweet scent sidled over to him, bringing back the unwelcome sympathy he'd felt for her last night when her father had dismissed her. His skin prickled with the awareness of her arm next to his.

Then his protective shield would slide back around him, slamming a barrier between him and his longings for Ashlyn.

Best thing, really. Ashlyn had too many strikes against her. Her innocence, her "Spencer-ness." But that didn't keep his gaze from straying to the curve of her breasts under a light sweater, the length of leg covered by faded jeans, the sunrise-tinted skin he'd caressed yesterday…

A sudden flash of light made him blink. Polka dots swam in front of his eyes as he heard Tag's laughter.

"Gotcha," said the kid.

Sam's gaze cleared enough for him to spot the dime-store disposable camera in Tag's grip.

Ashlyn said, "Sneaky, Taggert. Are you in paparazzo training?"

Tag tucked away his camera, ignoring the comment.

Sam reached out, bringing Tag to his lap for a good tickle. The kid tried to stifle his laughter. Smart. He didn't want to scare away the fish.

When Sam was tickled out, he paused, both of them breathing with the burst of energy. As they gathered strength, Sam realized that Tag felt natural here, leaning against him. Almost like a son of his own.

As Tag sighed and stood, Sam caught Ashlyn's

gaze, a wistful sheen covering the rainbows in her eyes. They both looked away.

The kid sighed. "This spot is no good. I'm going down the dock, sir."

"Stay in our sight." Damn, his voice sounded gruff, especially after having survived the shock of that zombie-morning camera shoot.

As Tag took a spot several yards down, yet within yelling range, Sam pulled up a knee to lean his arm on.

"I heard the latest rumor at the general store last night," Ashlyn said, her tone a mellow blend of musical notes and barely restrained amusement.

Maybe their silence had gotten to her, too.

"About what?"

"Rachel Shane." Her back straightened as she searched his face.

"That they found her husband? Yeah, I heard. Being sheriff means I get to hear a lot."

She paused, and it looked as if she was trying to read his mind. Sam shifted, scooted an inch away from her.

She said, "It's about time, isn't it? He'd been missing for over two years. I don't know what I would've done. It'll be interesting to see how she treats him when he comes back."

"If he comes back." From what Sam remembered of Matthew in high school, the man had fostered a real love of the wild life. Rumor had it that he'd continued that predilection for parties and women after his marriage. Not that it was any of Sam's business, but he wondered how a tough woman like Rachel had stood for it.

"At any rate, I'm happy for Rachel Shane," Ashlyn said.

Was her smile forced? It reeked of a woodenness Sam had never seen with her.

"What are you gaping at? Is something on my face?" she said, her fingers sneaking up to her mouth to wipe away imagined crumbs.

"Yeah, you've got something on your face. Egg."

Ashlyn grinned and seemed to catch on to his facetious game. "That's not even what I had for breakfast."

"I'd like to see you eat the truth for breakfast. Or lunch. Or dinner."

Ashlyn groaned. "Not again. I told you last night that I painted that wall."

"Tag says it was him."

"Then believe what you want. I'm obviously not going to change your opinion."

"I'm just a little worried about how Horatio Spencer treats his daughter." He shrank back, hardly believing he'd said the words. Too late. No chasing them down.

Ashlyn's hand fluttered to her necklace, skimmed over it, then returned to her pole. She couldn't believe Sam was interested. Was it too much to ask? Did he actually care about her in some deep, dark place in his soul?

Sam's next words seemed rushed. "Always a cop, huh? Worried about other people, poking my badge in everyone's housekeeping. I moved back to Kane's Crossing to cut back on that habit."

Of course. His concern was due to his instinct, his need to keep his townspeople safe. A good sheriff until the end. "Was it that taxing? Worrying about your charges in Washington, D.C., I mean."

He shrugged. "I didn't leave the city because of the stress. Not exactly. It all built up, I guess."

The sun threw flames across the water and they reached out to dab Sam's face with their orange and yellow shades. His brown hair looked darker in the subdued colors, giving him a relaxed air. She liked this version of Sam, this reclining man with a fishing pole dipping from his hand, a man who was actually talking some sense to her. She felt comfortable with him.

Not for the first time, she wondered what had happened to make him so melancholy. "Have you ever been happy, Sam?"

The candid question must have caught him off guard. For a moment she thought he wouldn't answer her. Then his shoulders relaxed.

"I guess I was happy when my parents were alive, when Nick lived with us. It wasn't a long stretch of time, but, by God, we were great brothers." He paused. "I suppose I was happy when I was married."

Her heart lurched forward. Married?

Heck, maybe she'd known about his marriage after all, heard it mentioned in passing before he'd come back to Kane's Crossing, but hearing him say it was painful. A dagger to the heart.

She tried to smile. "What was she like?"

During his hesitation, the water rippled, the tree leaves stirred, birds chirped good-morning tunes. "Mary taught kindergarten. She was so small I could fit my hands around her waist. And she was smart, too. Read a lot of books, went to a lot of lectures, just for the hell of it.''

The yearning in his voice made Ashlyn want to disappear like mist off the lake. Why had she asked him when she knew it was going to be painful to think of Sam loving another woman?

His words had dropped off to nothing.

Ashlyn took a deep breath. ''She didn't come to Kane's Crossing with you?''

''She died. Drunk driver, hit-and-run. You know the drill.''

Yes, every story in the newspaper had a face, but looking into this one was more hurtful than Ashlyn could have imagined. ''I'm sorry to hear that,'' she said.

''Yeah, well…'' He clamped his lips together.

Conversation over. Good thing, too. He'd loved his wife, Mary. Loved her a lot, as far as she could tell. He was so affected by her memory he couldn't even talk about it anymore.

Second place for life.

Right. Ashlyn Spencer was a walking red ribbon, a runner-up forever. She'd always been second place to her brother, so why was it so surprising that the same would hold true for Sam?

Obviously he'd always love Mary, and that was a good thing. Why would Ashlyn be interested in a man who wasn't capable of love anyway?

But she couldn't compete with a beloved ghost.

She needed to get a hold of herself, to give up all thoughts of flower ribbons and moonlit high-school kisses.

For her own good, Ashlyn needed to forget Sam Reno.

Chapter Eight

"You took Ashlyn Spencer fishing two days ago?" Nick asked, voice tense as barbed wire, while he and Sam sat on Nick's porch.

Sam rested his bottleneck beer against the wood of the sliding swing. "So?"

Nick's light blue gaze settled on his foster brother. "I wonder if you know what you're getting into."

"It's nothing."

"Yeah. Sounds like nothing."

Sam grimaced. "Leave it to a younger brother to know everything. Besides, your wife was the one who had the bright idea to team Ashlyn and me together with Tag."

"Leave Meggie out of it." Nick took a swig of beer.

Sam knew Meg could do no wrong in Nick's

eyes, so he dropped it. They sat in silence for a few minutes, each to his own thoughts. Sam didn't doubt that his sibling's head was filled with visions of Meg's curly red hair, his son and daughter, napping upstairs.

As for Sam's own musings… Hell, they could stay in the back of his mind where they belonged. But he couldn't help remembering the feel of Ashlyn's soft lips, the lackadaisical freedom of her out-of-bed hair.

Nick gestured toward the burned-out sun with his bottle. "Sunsets aren't the same anywhere else on earth as they are in Kentucky, are they, Sam?"

He shrugged. "I haven't noticed."

"You will." Nick paused, then added, "You have the hots for that Ashlyn?"

"Hell, no."

"Yeah, that's what I thought." A long swallow from his beer. "Now I don't pay much attention to gossip, but you should know that people are talking."

"About what?"

"About you two lovebirds, that's what."

This couldn't be true. Just because he and Ashlyn had been spending a lot of time with Tag—together and apart—that didn't mean they were…that he was…

Sam shifted position, the swing creaking with his weight. "You of all people should know that I wouldn't get involved with Ashlyn Spencer."

Nick's voice lowered, scratching over Sam's conscience.

"Listen, I promised Meggie I'd get over my hate, because when I came back to Kane's Crossing, I was full of it. I had to learn the difference between justice and revenge. Meggie taught me, and that's why I owe her the world.''

Nick hesitated, assessing Sam, then continued. ''I know you still hold a lot of anger against the Spencers, Sam. But you're going to have to ask yourself if it's worth your energy. And it's not, I'll tell you that much.''

Sam felt the shaking start in the core of him, a quiet quake that had consumed his life for the past seven years. He'd tried so hard to forget it. ''Dammit, Nick, I can't forgive that family for what they did to us. Are you telling me you've wiped the slate clean between you and Chad Spencer? Has it slipped your memory that he's the guy who framed you for setting off a bomb?''

''It's in the past.'' Hard edges bracketed Nick's mouth.

Sam cursed. ''Admit it. Deep inside, the pain hasn't dulled, has it?'' Once again, he wondered if it had mellowed in his own soul. If it mattered so much, why hadn't he let his rage loose over Horatio Spencer when he had the chance?

Was this so-called hatred just an excuse to distance himself from the process of living?

Nick sighed. ''Yeah, the Spencers hurt us, okay? But I've let go of the hatred. I'd be crazy not to since I've got everything I need in Meggie and the kids.'' Nick's brow smoothed as he watched his brother. ''I just don't want to see you torn up by your feelings for the Spencers. It's not worth the cost.''

Sam didn't know whether his soul was burning with anger, or numb with hatred. Before Meg's influence, Nick had set out to gain revenge on the Spencers. But Sam had skipped right over the revenge part of it and gone to the dead zone, where it hurt less to think about his life.

And that's what he'd have to do with Ashlyn—go to the dead zone. She'd been stirring up too many emotions in him, feelings he'd vowed to steer clear of. Sam would keep his sanity only if he managed to push caring aside. Caring hurt too much.

Nick said, "Don't let your bitterness sneak up on you, Sam. Just be aware."

He was more aware than he wanted to be. Aware of her smile, of her sexy legs, of her warm lips parted to cushion an ill-advised kiss.

"You're not listening to a word I say, are you?" Nick watched his brother intently.

Sam just took a sip of beer. A big one.

"Damn, Sam. Ashlyn's a good enough person, I suppose, but I don't want to see you hurting. Not like you were when I found you in D.C."

"I know."

Nick cursed under his breath. "Do what you will, you cantankerous rock."

Sam closed his eyes, wishing he had the libido of a rock. It'd sure as hell help him where Ashlyn was concerned.

Across town, Ashlyn strolled past Meg's bakery one more time, attempting to seem casual. She'd been working in her studio, sketching ideas for her silver jewelry, when she felt a sudden craving for Meg's blueberry "boyfriend" pie.

What harm would come of a bite? she'd thought. But the more Ashlyn thought about it, the more she remembered the way Sam kept his distance from her.

She ran her fingertips over her lips, the fire of Sam's kiss still singeing her. Not even the space of a few days had allowed her to forget the scratch of his cheek, the pulse of his mouth against hers.

It'd take time to forget her crush, she knew. The trick was to stay away from Sam, to escape his body heat, the memory of his towering shadow.

Ashlyn peeked through the lettering on the bakery window again, hoping no one in the crowd would catch her staring, contemplating that darned blueberry pie.

The door clanged open with the ring of bells. Meg Cassidy smiled out at Ashlyn, her hair piled loosely in a mound of saucy curls. "Are you coming in?"

Ashlyn's cheeks heated up. *Admit it,* she thought, *Meg's here a few days a week. You were hoping she'd be in today.*

"I guess I could spare a moment," Ashlyn said.

She ducked through the doorway, following Meg to the Formica-topped counter. A Buddy Holly song played over the aroma of chocolate, apples and pastries.

Meg scooted behind the counter, retying her apron, as Ashlyn perched on a stool, ordering a cup of jasmine tea and a slice of strawberry pie.

"Are you sure you don't want blueberry?" Meg asked, a glint in her green eyes.

Was Ashlyn that obvious? Even so, she knew her pride wouldn't allow her to order a slice. "Not today, though I hear you've been baking them feverishly."

"True," Meg said. She filled Ashlyn's cup and

scooped a slice of pie onto a plate as she talked. "When I'm here, I can't keep up. Widow Antle refuses to bake them."

"That's because everyone expects your magic touch," Ashlyn said, referring to Meg's "witchy" reputation.

Blueberry pie, win your guy…

The town used to recite such rhymes about Meg's and her aunt Valentine's baking skills. Ashlyn didn't know how the young bride had kept her head up among all the mean-spirited gossip.

Meg leaned against the counter, smiling at the two employees who helped the customers. "So, how's life treating you, Ashlyn? I notice you and Sam have been spending a lot of time with Taggert."

Ashlyn's soul lit up with thoughts of the brown-eyed boy. "Yeah. If I ever have a child, I'd like him to be just like Tag."

"He adores you, too. And I think you and Sam are getting along just swimmingly."

"I wouldn't go that far." Forget it. Steer the conversation away from him. "You know, Tag's so great because I don't have any reputation with him. He accepts me for who I am."

Meg laid a warm hand over Ashlyn's. "Who wouldn't?"

Ashlyn didn't want to whip out her mile-long list of people.

Touched by Meg's comfort, Ashlyn squeezed her fingers. "Wouldn't it be nice if we could all be regular people, without pasts?"

"Well, if my husband, the world's most stubborn man, can forget about former lives, maybe the rest of the town can, as well. Maybe it's worth a try."

"Nice pipe dream, huh?" Ashlyn grinned and absently plunged a chunk of pie into her mouth. The strawberries tasted like sun shining on a summer field, like red temptation packed into a pastry-tinged bite. She sighed in near ecstasy. "You are incredible, Meg."

She'd been so immersed in avoiding Meg's gaze that, when she looked at her, Ashlyn was surprised to see Meg gnawing her lip. Looked like a prelude to a scheme.

"You're plotting something wicked," Ashlyn said.

"Oh, don't be so suspicious," Meg said. "Would you like to join us for dinner tonight, up at the house?"

Ashlyn almost jumped out of her seat. Ever since she was old enough to appreciate a good scare, she'd been eager to see the inside of Meg's Gothic-featured home. "Wouldn't Nick be a tad put out with you?"

"Oh, never mind him. Nick likes you, he just won't admit it. And you can see the twins."

The unspoken memory of town gossip hung between them. Even if the twins weren't Chad's children, Ashlyn had a soft spot for them anyway. The fact that Meg was offering to let Ashlyn see them, in spite of all her trouble in keeping their paternity a secret during the past couple of years, touched Ashlyn.

How could she refuse?

"If you think Nick won't be angry with you, then, yes, I'd love to come over for dinner."

Meg nodded. "Wonderful. Sam's going to be

there, too, but you should be used to him by now,
what with your fishing trips and haircuts.''

Ashlyn wanted to take back her dinner acceptance
and run out the door with it. ''Maybe Sam needs a
break from me.''

''Don't be silly, Ashlyn. I think we can all get
along like adults.''

She wanted to tell Meg that Nick and Sam would
probably never forgive her, but Meg was a smart
woman. She knew what she was doing.

Ashlyn hoped.

Meg started to walk away. ''Just let me finish
with a couple of pies, and I'll drive us home. I just
got my license.''

Ashlyn thought of what Sam's face would look
like when she walked through Meg and Nick's door.

Even if this was a bad idea, she couldn't wait to
see him again.

Ever since Meg had squealed up the long driveway in her gently used Coupe Deville, the night had
been unbearable for Sam.

First, Meg had brushed through the stained-glass
foyer, kissed Nick and the twins hello, dragging
Ashlyn Spencer right along with her. Sam and Nick
had exchanged glances, but Sam had acted as if
Ashlyn's presence didn't matter a bit to him.

When, of course, it did.

His body was still throbbing with the sight of
Ashlyn in a long-sleeved sweater that hugged her
body, the hem of it cropped above her belly button.
A well-worn pair of pants hugged her hips as a thin,
silver belly chain circled her trim waist.

He wanted to reach out, run his hands over the

flat planes of her stomach, hooking his thumbs into that web strand of a belly chain, dipping his fingers into the back waistband of her pants to feel the warmth of her skin. He wanted to explore the small of her back, tickling the tiny down hairs that shined like silk threads in the candlelight.

Sam sat upright at the dinner table, trying to tell himself that Ashlyn's eyes didn't glimmer like a kaleidoscope every time the candleflames flickered. He tried to tell himself that her sun-kissed cheeks weren't begging to be skimmed by his fingertips.

But it was no good. Meg obviously knew that he was attracted to Ashlyn Spencer, even if he wouldn't admit it himself.

No more hurt. No more pain. *Dead zone.*

Laughter rang out between Meg and Ashlyn at the other end of the mahogany dining room table as they fed the twins crushed peas. Nick wrinkled his forehead while he concentrated on shoveling lasagna, salad and garlic bread into his mouth. Sam couldn't eat, he was so damned ticked.

His gaze met Meg's, and Sam frowned, televising his discomfort with her dinner plans. Ashlyn seemed oblivious to it all, koo-chi-cooing with little Valerie and Jake, wiping stray vegetable matter off the children's' chins, smoothing auburn curls away from shining blue eyes.

She was a natural with kids. Tag adored her, the twins couldn't stop giggling at her musical laughter and spirited clowning. The man who ended up marrying her would have a happy household.

Sam clenched his jaw and averted his gaze, glancing instead at the baroque dining room, the ornate woodwork lining the ceiling and walls, the velvet burgundy wallpaper reflecting flames from the low fire in the grate. The tomato-and-mozzarella aroma of the lasagna mixed with an elusive magnolia scent further adding to Sam's discomfort.

Meg cleared her throat, too loudly to be casual. All eyes fastened on her.

"Are you boys taking Neanderthal lessons from the other men in town?"

Nick's head shot up, lips half open, a slice of bread poised to be stuffed into his mouth.

Sam shifted in his chair, feeling chastised. He noticed that Ashlyn's attention was still focused on the kids in their high chairs, as if she knew that she was the reason he and Nick were agitated.

Meg continued, her voice low, as soothing and deceptive as a lullaby. "Now I'm not going to lose my temper here, in front of my children, but we all need to get something straight. I'm through with playing this town's games. We're better than that. If any of you men would care to treat our dinner guest with some of the respect she deserves, please feel free. If not, then go out back to the garden where I feed the wild things."

Nick gulped down the last of his food, sitting back in his chair to shoot Sam an amused glance. Sam folded his arms across his chest, feeling the edges of his badge rub against his skin.

Ashlyn watched her half-full plate, a blush pinking her cheeks. Sam almost felt sorry for her. But not quite.

Meg continued her lethal eye contact, making Sam feel as though he'd just been taken behind the woodshed for a good whooping.

"This town is ready for a change," she said.

"Wouldn't it be nice if we could forget that Ashlyn is a Spencer and we're from the other side of the tracks? We've got a real chance to usher in some peace. Some happiness. What's done is done, and I don't believe dredging up old grievances and hurts is going to do us any good. Keep in mind that Ashlyn was my maid of honor. And I didn't take that favor lightly."

Ashlyn smiled at Meg, who returned the gesture.

Nick sighed, reached for his beer, took a swig during a considering pause. "So what do we talk about, Meggie?"

"What do normal folks talk about?"

"If we were normal, I'd have a better idea."

Sam just wanted to leave, amble right out the door where he couldn't catch a whiff of Ashlyn's shampoo-clean scent, where he couldn't obsess over the lips he'd tasted days before.

She stood, brushing off her pants. "It'd probably be best if I made myself scarce."

Before Meg could speak, Nick beat her to it. "No, have a seat. You don't deserve my cold shoulder, Ashlyn. Never did."

She smiled again, this time at Nick, who looked as if he'd rather be sticking toothpicks under his thumbnails.

A spotlight seemed to descend over Sam; a moment in which everyone waited for him to second Nick's opinion.

He glanced around the table, noting Meg's and Nick's expectant demeanors. Even the twins had stopped messing around with their food to gape at him.

He didn't crack a smile. "Is this where we all collapse into a group hug?"

His brother and sister-in-law both stared at him in disbelief.

Ashlyn, on the other hand, threw back her head, laughing. "Leave it to you, Sam," she said.

Sam's body tightened as his gaze skimmed down the soft skin of her throat, the smoothness of her breasts. They seemed plump enough to warm his cupped hands. Sam could imagine circling their fullness with his thumb, coaxing them to hardness.

He throbbed in places that hadn't experienced such intense action for a while.

A sigh finished off Ashlyn's laugh, and she sat back down, a different, happier person. "That relieved the tension."

Meg rolled her eyes and stood, untying her daughter's bib.

"Nick, let's take the kids upstairs." She turned to Sam and Ashlyn. "You both are welcome to stay. We can start up the fireplace in the living room."

Sam rose from his chair, as well. "After I help you clean up here, I'd better get going, check on Deputy Joanson at the office. You never know what kind of crisis is developing with him on watch."

Meg laughed. "Hear that, Nick? Maybe you can visit Gary Joanson, too."

Nick's face flamed, but he stayed silent as Ashlyn joined Meg in laughing. The whole town knew how much the impressionable deputy admired Nick. Gary had latched on to him with the tenacity of a panting dog over the past two years, probably because of the way Nick had given a sense of freedom to Kane's Crossing. As a result, Gary had become his own person, breaking away from the town-bully group to become a deputy *and* a doting father.

Ashlyn grabbed a few plates. ''I need to leave, too. So much to accomplish in our short lives, you know.''

Was she mocking him somehow? He gathered silverware and cups, moving to the kitchen to avoid additional conversation, lighthearted talk that would reveal more than he wanted anyone to know.

Meg followed. ''Never mind cleaning, Sam, we've got it. Hey, are you okay?''

''I'm fine.''

She laid a hand on his arm. ''I'm sorry for putting you in a hard position. I was wrong to do it.''

''Actually, Meg, you were right. Even if I'm not up to it.''

''You are. You'll see.'' She took his tableware and laid it carefully in the sink. ''One more favor?''

He bristled at her smile. ''What?''

''Drive Ashlyn home? She doesn't have her car.''

''Hell, why not,'' he mumbled, chasing away the side of him that was doing cartwheels at the suggestion. ''I'm kind of getting used to chauffeuring her around.''

Something in Meg's eyes said, ''You're getting used to a lot of things about Ashlyn Spencer.'' But maybe it was his conscience reflected right back at him.

Ashlyn walked in with the dish of leftover lasagna. Meg took it from her, refusing any more cleaning help.

''Don't worry about us. Sam's driving you home.''

"Driving?" Ashlyn said. "Heck, I'm walking. It's beautiful out there."

Sam's guard went up. "Haven't we talked about this before, Ashlyn?"

"Sure, we have. And I remember pointing out that this is Kane's Crossing. It's not exactly the crime capital of the nation."

"No, that's where I'm from." Sam grabbed their coats from the nearby rack. "Humor me?"

Ashlyn grinned at him, sending Fourth-of-July-sparkler nips over his skin.

"I'm not wasting this night, Sam." She turned to Meg. "Thank you for dinner. It was great."

Meg hugged her, then Sam. She whispered, "I used to walk all over Kane's Crossing before Nick came back. Don't worry. She can take care of herself."

A guilt trip was mapped all over his better judgment. He wasn't about to let Ashlyn walk by herself in the dark of night. Not after the things he'd seen in Washington, D.C.

Sam shrugged into his jacket. "Thank you for everything, Meg. Ashlyn, let's go."

She'd already buttoned her coat to the chin. "But—"

He tried not to growl. Why was he doing this? "We can walk. And don't say another word."

Ashlyn pursed her lips together, forming two little dimples in the corners of that mouth.

Sam only hoped he'd be strong enough to avoid its lure tonight.

Chapter Nine

For the tail end of April, the weather had been kind, Ashlyn thought, trying to steady her breathing as she matched Sam Reno's long steps.

Gnarled shade from a looming elm tree shadowed his face from the moonlight, hiding his emotions.

As if she needed to see his eyes to know what was probably running through his mind. "Sam, if you don't want to walk, go to your car. I don't need an escort."

He glanced over his shoulder at Nick and Meg's "house on haunted hill," now a dark speck against the skyline. "How much farther?"

"I know a shortcut. It's really not a great distance between the Cassidys and the Spencers." She wished the same were true in the philosophical sense.

A path cut through the grass to their right.

"Here," she said, tugging his sleeve for him to follow her. "This shaves off about twenty minutes."

She imagined he was thinking that it was still too much time for him to be dragging her home.

Sam shot past her at a fast clip, causing Ashlyn to expend all the energy she had to keep up with him. Was he racing the wind so he could get away from her? Did he sense, right along with her, that if they paused for only a second, they'd end up kissing again?

Bad idea. Maybe they could get along as acquaintances, but kissing, caressing, aching for more was completely out of the question.

Heat shot through Ashlyn's body as she lingered behind him, appreciating his massive height, the breadth of his back, the fit of his jeans. He was solid through and through, edges as rough hewn as a wood-carved sculpture.

He forged ahead, spring grass and post-winter foliage crisping under his boots. In the near distance, the old drive-in's screen loomed like a forgotten storm front, its canvas ripped away at the upper corner.

In the empty spaces where teenagers used to park steamy-windowed cars, lone speaker poles stood guard over a junkyard of sorts. Stuffing shot out of unbalanced, dirt-spotted sofas; an abandoned oven reclined in a perpetually surprised daze, its door depending on one hinge to hold open its gaping hole of a mouth. Ancient cars—tireless, windowless and rust-painted—stood audience to a movie that would never play again.

Ashlyn stopped, leaning against the property's

rickety wooden fence. "Shoot, Sam, where's the emergency?"

He paused, turned around, hands on hips. "I don't have the patience for this, Ashlyn."

What was he running from?

She blew out a breath, knowing that arguing with him wouldn't do any good. Clouds danced over the moon, loosing a blanket of silvery light over the landscape. She couldn't help smiling.

"What now?" Sam asked.

She nodded toward the sky. "There's a man in the moon."

"By, God. Would you come on?"

"No, really." She pushed off the fence to stand by him, reveling in the dark heat of his body. "Look closely. You can see his foolish grin, his big eyes and nose. Pretty clownlike."

A minute passed as Sam peered upward, his face showing no obvious feeling. Ashlyn's heart sank. Was he completely empty inside?

"There's nothing there. Let's go," he said.

"I suppose you don't catch much, what with your crusty attitude."

His brow furrowed. "Meaning what?"

"Meaning that you must lead a colorless life, Sam Reno. Don't you ever catch a snowflake to see why it's different from the others? Don't you look inside trees to see if fairies live inside?"

At his blank expression, she tossed up her hands. "I give up."

Then he watched her with clear worry. "You're talking to me about fairies."

"I know," she said, laughing to herself. "I sound like a starry-eyed kid, but, right now, I don't mind.

And I'm not even literally talking about fairies and gremlins and all the things that go bump in the night. I'm talking about miracles, those common everyday things we take for granted. Things Janey Trainor probably appreciated when she found out about her breast cancer—'' Her words choked off.

Now she felt really young, too idealistic in the face of his obvious cynicism. "Never mind."

"I think I might have looked at life that way, a long time ago."

He'd said it so softly, Ashlyn wasn't even sure she'd heard it. She held her breath, wondering if any disruption would stop him from talking.

But he didn't say anything more.

"When?" she asked, goading him on.

"Damn, I don't know. Maybe when I first got married, when, on our honeymoon, I looked at Mary's veil while she was dressing. I guess that was like snowflakes, you know, all the lace in those patterns. I wondered how someone could make those tiny pictures, how they could spend so much time on something no one ever pays attention to."

The wisp of a smile had tilted his lips, killing Ashlyn with its tenderness.

But you're still second place, she thought.

Second place.

He snapped out of his momentary reverie. "Aw, damn. Why even think about that nonsense?"

"Why not?" She wished she could describe the fleeting serenity she'd seen ghost over his face, wished she had the ability to make him feel that way, too.

"Waste of time," he said.

She couldn't hold back her next words. "I just

wish I could be that happy with someone, some-day.''

He knifed a tortured glare at her, his eyes burning with cold fires, no doubt newly banked by her thoughtless sentiments.

''I'm sorry,'' she said.

With that he looked away, at the ground, at his Doc Martens, which still gleamed city-boy new. ''Do me a favor. Let's not talk about it again.''

She nodded, her throat aching.

Ashlyn walked back to the fence, leaning her forearms between the pickets, staring at the deserted machinery and household items, feeling just as alone and gutted.

''Hey,'' he said. His boots crunched over the grass. ''Now I have to apologize.''

His voice was so low, so soft, rubbing over her like grains of warm sand.

She swallowed, trying to ignore the whisp of his jacket and shirt, the smell of woodsy-clean on his skin.

Concentrate on something besides Sam Reno, she told herself.

Her stare locked on to a '36 Ford Deluxe Cabri-olet, thinking about the artwork she'd accomplished while lounging in its front seat. ''Sometimes, when I want to get away from everyone, I come out here. I like to hang out in that car.'' She pointed to the Ford.

''Why am I not surprised at your creativity?'' he said.

His tone had lightened, causing her to hope that

their conversation could be more civil and less angst-filled.

"Well, you know, my first crush influenced me."

He chuckled dryly. "Why am I afraid to ask? All right, what the hell. Who was that man of your dreams?"

Ashlyn hesitated. "You have to understand, I was only about five."

"Spit it out."

She tented her fingers over her eyes. "Speed Racer."

Silence. Ashlyn looked out of the corner of her gaze, wanting to know if he'd walked away yet.

But he hadn't. He was still next to her, an entertained slant to his grin. "I thought you'd be more the Racer X type. You know, the mysterious big brother?"

"You were a fan of the show? Trixie, Mach Five, that scary little monkey..."

Sam backed away. "Hey, take it easy. I just watched it in my pajamas when I was a kid. I didn't fantasize about a cartoon person."

Ashlyn turned around to face Sam. "Then who was your first crush?"

Jo Ann Walters, his perfect rose-gifted girlfriend? Nah. Sam had been at least sixteen when they'd dated. But she wanted to ask about the cheerleader, wanted to know how much she'd meant to him.

For better or worse, she wanted to know everything about Sam Reno, even what made his eyes turn into a doomsday explosion every time she said the wrong words.

She wanted it all.

* * *

Sam turned the question over in his mind. He could hardly remember his first crush. "I guess I had a thing for Princess Leia."

"What little boy didn't?"

Sam shrugged. "I admit, she's no Speed Racer. Zero points for originality."

Ashlyn laughed, making him feel better than he'd felt in…well, a long time. Her laughter made him think of carousel music—fantasy-filled tunes tinted with energy and happiness.

She was so beautiful it made his chest ache. And it made something even more sinister claw at his insides, hungering to get out.

He leaned nearer to her, his body controlling every don't-you-dare scream of his mind. "What about your cartoon-driven fantasies? Did you ever get over Speed's jaunty red scarf and unparalleled moxy?"

Her breaths came in short gasps, and she tried to cover it with more laughter. But it wasn't fooling him, or her, judging from her widened eyes.

"I kinda dug Greg Brady."

Sam couldn't help chuckling—long, rob-your-breath lightness that made him want to pull her into his arms to be protected from her own self.

"Unbelievable," he said between laughs.

She caught the giggle bug, as well, and they both slumped on the fence. After a few minutes, tears streamed down her face she was laughing so hard.

Sam reached out to wipe them away, cutting short the gaiety. Ashlyn hitched in a breath and seemed to hold it until he removed his touch.

But seconds later, he couldn't help touching her again.

He moved his fingertips down her face, feeling the hollow of her cheek, the edge of her lips. She bowed her head as he reached her neck, running his fingernails over her veins, then scooping up his palms to frame her jaw, pulling her face near his.

She stumbled over her words. "You know what you're doing?"

He ignored the implications. "Damned straight."

Last time he'd barely brushed her mouth with his, tasting a forbidden luxury. This time he took full advantage of the moon dappling the need in her eyes. Their lips connected, heat ignited by a yearning set to explode. She tasted of sun bursting over a rainy day, of almond and honey mixed together—sweet, hot, heady.

She traced her fingers in his hair, making him feel as brain-addled as she had in the barbershop when she'd taken the broom to his shoulders, whisking against his shirt, tingling his skin with longing. He hadn't allowed himself to enjoy her touch then, but nothing was stopping him now.

Nothing.

Guilt knocked at the back of his mind, but he blocked it out when her hands palmed down his neck, under his lawman's jacket and over his chest, the pads of her fingers playing near his ribs.

He wanted to lower them both to the grass, to erase his need by giving in to it, slipping off her clothes, slipping into her.

Sam heard himself groan as she caressed his back, and he leaned down to get closer, to run his fingers through her short, soft hair, to ease his tongue and lips over her throat and into the soft groove behind her ear.

Ashlyn stirred under him, coaxing Sam to move

closer, meld his body to hers. The length of her legs were a nice match for his, he thought as one twined around the back of him.

When he smoothed a hand over her breast—soft and full as a cloud should feel—Ashlyn cupped a hand over his, urging him on, making him crazier than he had any right to be.

Then the memories of past heartache reintroduced themselves, dragging him away, dousing him with a cold shower of guilt.

He backed away, trying to not allow Ashlyn's hurt gaze be his undoing.

She sighed heavily, clutching her coat around her body. "I know, I know. That should've never happened."

Sam wanted to tell her that it might have happened if his memories hadn't kicked in.

How could he tell her why he'd stopped? He couldn't stand her embarrassment, her natural assumption that he'd pulled away because she was a Spencer, something she could never change.

Thing was, her Spencer-ness hadn't entered into the process at all. His unwillingness to get closer to her was *his* problem.

"Ashlyn, this has nothing to do with you."

She crossed her arms over her chest. "Then what is it?"

As he searched for something to say, realization eclipsed her, darkening her once-bright eyes. "Your wife? You're still in love with your wife."

He couldn't respond. A misspent year and a half should have erased his inability to move on with his life after Mary's death, but it hadn't. And now Ashlyn would suffer because of it.

Sam watched Ashlyn step away, admiring her pride. Wanting her to stay, even if he couldn't explain why he'd stopped the kiss.

He didn't understand it, either.

"Go home, Sam," she said, walking away. "Just go home."

He watched her leave, wishing he had the strength to call her back.

But thoughts of pain kept him silent and faithful.

The next day, the only thing that could keep Ashlyn's mind off Sam was something catastrophic. And fate gladly provided her with that something.

Reports of a Spenco factory shutdown had chimed over her car radio early this afternoon, almost flooding out memories of Sam leaning down to press his mouth to hers, Sam running his hands over her body, leaving her helplessly willing for more.

But this was a nightmare. The news had been false, a runaway rumor, but Ashlyn knew that the whole town would be reeling with memories of the big accident—the one that had killed ten people, plus Sam's dad.

After hearing the first newscast, Ashlyn had driven to the toy factory to check on her father, who wasn't available to talk to anyone. He'd been too busy putting out publicity fires, said his secretary, assuring Ashlyn that she needn't worry.

She'd driven back to town, almost afraid to look the citizens of Kane's Crossing in the eye. Were they thinking about the old accident, as well?

As she drove to Sam's office, faint flashes of memory assaulted her. A glint of metal machinery, a burst of explosive light, rocks cutting off sunlight streaming into the cave, screams...

"Cut it out," she told herself, her teeth grinding together.

She passed the Reno Center, noticing Nick Cassidy sliding out of his road-worn red pickup parked in front. While pulling into the sheriff's lot, she saw the Bronco sitting in its place of honor by the door. She was willing to bet Sam was in.

Not for the first time, she wondered if this was such a great idea—to talk to him about the rumors. She knew what he'd be thinking, that he'd be hot under the collar about the Spencers and their greedy factory, but she felt the need to clear the air before it affected their relationship with Tag. Ashlyn didn't want the little boy to suffer because his Big Brother and Big Sister couldn't get along.

And, actually, she didn't want to suffer, either. Better to talk about this now before it became a problem.

She took a deep breath, whipped off her fifties-fashioned sunglasses and slid them into her jeans' pocket. Then she walked into the station.

Oddly enough, the office was quiet. The radio sat on the desk, silent, and no one seemed to be around.

"Hello?" she asked.

Heavy footfalls preceded Sam's appearance. When he rounded the corner to his desk, a faint spark crossed his eyes then sputtered out, leaving him to stare at her as if she'd come back from the dead.

"How can I help you?"

Cop talk. Great. She wanted last night's Sam back, even if she had told him to go home.

"I think you know why I'm here," she said.

"Do we really need to talk about this?" He sat in his chair, attacking the scant paperwork on his desk.

"Yes, we do. Would you listen to me? I want to talk about what happened at the factory today."

He held up his hands, barring her words from getting to him. "I already went up there to investigate, Ashlyn."

"So you know nothing's wrong?"

"I think we both know the answer to that."

She plopped back against the wall, her posture wilting. "I know. You're thinking of your father and what happened seven years ago—"

"—I'm thinking of idiotic choices and how I'll never make them again."

He'd turned to look at her once more, his large hands—the ones that had held her just last night— clutching the edge of his desk. The huge slab seemed like miles to cross before she could get to him.

"Sam," she said softly, wishing she could understand. "I have no idea what you're talking about."

"Let's put it this way. Once you allow someone to take advantage of your faith in them, you'll never let it happen again."

She must have seemed confused, because he went on, his voice cut with barely contained agony.

"Now is a good time to tell you one of the reasons I came back to Kane's Crossing. I was a patrol cop, and I thought I'd seen it all until this one day…" He stared through her. "These kids were walking home from school and… I won't fool you, this was a part of the city that lies off the beaten tourist paths. Not the picture-perfect photo ops you'd come to expect from D.C. These kids walked past this house. It looked ordinary from the outside, but, inside… You know what a meth lab is?''

Ashlyn shook her head.

"Methamphetimine. The greediest men in the world can create this drug from household items. They use regular houses to disguise the labs, the places where they cook the meth. It's a powerful drug, and very volatile during the cooking process.''

He stopped, as if remembering something he wanted to erase from his mind's eye. "Evidently the chemistry wasn't right that day because the house exploded. It happens more than you think, and you can never tell which house contains a lab. These kids didn't know. No one in the neighborhood knew. The crooks were new tenants, living next door to people who would work two jobs to stay off welfare, people who tried to earn a clean living and keep their kids safe.''

Ashlyn knew what was coming next, didn't know if she wanted to hear it. "The kids were hurt as they walked by?''

"I found a shoe,'' Sam said, his expression stone-like. "We found the rest of them farther away from the house.''

"Oh, God.''

Sam stood, a cage of anger surrounding him, causing Ashlyn to want to back away.

"I'm not telling you this fairy tale so you'd feel sorry for me. I'm going to make a point. I'd run into the cook before. He'd been arrested for the same damned thing but, when he went to trial, his attorney pulled something fancy and got him off the hook, back on the streets. Afterward, I had a chat with him while I was on patrol. Oh, yeah, he was so sorry, so repentant. And I was green enough to believe this guy would never cook again. I was even willing to give him another chance when I saw that he'd rented a cozy house, the one he ultimately blew to smithereens during his meth cooking. 'Everyone is entitled to a second chance,' I thought. 'Leave him alone.'''

"You couldn't have done anything."

Sam clenched his fists. "Maybe, maybe not. But I could have predicted what his greed would get him into. Greed is the same disease in everyone, does the same damage. I learned to never give greed a second chance. Never again."

A red film settled over Ashlyn's eyes. She started to shiver, a deep stomach-trembling lack of control that carried over to her voice. "What are you insinuating?"

"You're an intelligent woman, so there's really no need to ask. I made the choice to believe the best about people. That choice killed my instincts, and I'm never going to make the same decision again."

"You're equating my father to these meth criminals?"

The radio squealed, dragging out the tense moment.

After the noise died down, Sam turned away from her. "You're the one who figured it out, Ashlyn. Greed is greed."

Was she hearing him correctly? Sam Reno, passing such harsh judgment on her family? This couldn't have been the same man who'd felt so right against her last night. "My father is hardly a criminal, Sheriff Reno. Maybe he's a little ambitious, but he's not a child-killing monster."

Sam's silence said everything. Horatio Spencer didn't murder children—he'd murdered Sam's father.

She felt frustration take the form of tears, burning her throat with their protestations. "You're so blinded by hate, Sam Reno, that you wouldn't be able to determine the truth if it spit at you. And it's a stubborn hate you have, cold and deaf. Now I'm sorry about this morning's scare, but don't think for a minute that my family is enjoying all the pain it's bringing back to this town. And to you."

She left his office before he could see the tears.

Before she'd lost the last of her strength in front of a man whose opinion meant more to her than she wanted to admit.

Chapter Ten

"Why are there so many boxes?" Tag asked Sam later that night in Sam's family room.

It was three hours after the kid had crept into the station once again. At the end of his wire, Sam had started to walk Tag back to the Reno Center, but not before the child had talked him into calling the reception desk so they could hang out. Sam had grudgingly given in to Tag's whim, picking up some fried chicken from the market and taking the kid home for dinner.

Sam glanced around the empty space, a gray-carpeted area dotted with cardboard luggage. He still hadn't bothered to unpack, to settle in with the left-over furniture.

He shuffled some paper plates to the floor while Tag opened the various bags filled with mashed potatoes, biscuits, gravy and coleslaw. "Would you rather eat outside?" Sam asked.

"Yup." The eight-year-old perked up his chin at the sound of gravel crunching under tires in the driveway.

Sam turned to Tag, wondering what the ruckus was all about. But the kid had already scooted out the door, leaving Sam with the food and the frustration that had lingered all day. Ever since Ashlyn had come to the station.

Now that Tag had left him alone, Sam felt like punching something, but he talked himself out of it.

Cool, calm, detached. That's how he moved through life, never allowing the world around him to touch his emotions, never letting hurt creep in and hide in his soul, allowing it to torture him during the night.

Sam walked to the window, the filmy lace of the last owner's abandoned curtains almost blocking his view.

Ashlyn. Outside. Hugging Tag hello.

The last time he'd seen her had been merely hours ago, when she'd been dabbing at her eyes, when she'd slipped on sunglasses and backed out of the sheriff's office parking lot.

Yeah, Sam, you're a real piece of work, he'd thought. But what was he supposed to do—woo her with soft words and promises of forever?

Right. He knew he'd spoken harshly to her earlier—too harshly—but that was because his memories had roughened his spirit and beat him down. All Sam knew was that greed had raised the Spenco factory from the dead, and it was back to do more damage, to enliven his memories and his need for the truth.

Besides, it wasn't Ashlyn's fault that her father wanted money at any cost.

There he went again, getting all soft. Just because he couldn't get his fool mind off of last night and the kiss they'd shared didn't mean he needed to apologize to her. Or did it?

Maybe treating her like a human being instead of a criminal's daughter would be a good idea. And he'd certainly have the opportunity to try.

Tag pulled Ashlyn toward the door, but she tugged on the kid's hand, hanging back as her gaze scanned his home. Sam wondered if she didn't want to see him, if she'd turn tail and run.

Sam stepped away from the window, opened the screened door and walked onto the porch.

When Ashlyn saw him, she stopped, tilting her head in apparent challenge. "Meg said Tag was with you. I promised to take him to the Barkley Buffet tonight."

"We have chicken," Sam said, hating the inadequacy of the explanation. What he wanted to say was, "I guess I'm sorry for what I said this afternoon."

Sure. He had too much pride in his family to admit he might be going a little hard on the Spencers.

"Fried chicken?" she asked. "How fattening."

Tag smiled up at her. "You can eat the runny *cold slawn.*"

She ruffled Tag's dark hair before he sprinted into the house. "Sounds delightful."

Alone again. Nothing to say as they stared past each other.

When he flashed a glance at her once more she was considering his house. He noticed that her expression matched the one she'd worn last night when she'd talked to him about snowflakes and fairies—full of wonder in small miracles.

He stepped closer to her, wondering if the rich girl in Ashlyn felt sorry for the house his limited budget had purchased. "It's not much, but it's home," he said.

The last word sounded as hollow as eternity to him, but she stayed smiling.

Then he realized what she was seeing. *His* home, a statement of who he was. A modest, maybe even decent structure, as plain-spoken as its owner.

Hell, come to think of it, he'd never really looked at his own house before. Maybe he should look at it, too. See what she was seeing.

With a tentative shrug, he turned around, taking in the white-clapboard-Americana sturdiness of it.

He'd never noticed the Tom Sawyer-bright paint, the soft lights glowing through lace curtains, the hum of a silent, falling night settling over a freshly shingled roof.

The beauty of it reached out to choke him. He was almost ashamed when Ashlyn whispered, "It's perfect."

And it was, with the murmuring spray of a busted hose faucet by the wide-armed porch; the tire swing creaking from a rope tied to an oak that had been around to spin tales from the days of antebellum barbecues and Dixie-whistling Southern nights. The stalwart tree had probably even heard the low, sad song of a scythe as it whistled through a nearby field.

How could he not have recognized each detail?

He cleared his throat, embarrassed by his stopping-to-smell-the-roses attitude. "Come in for dinner."

"And I suppose we're going to pretend we didn't have that conversation this afternoon," she said.

"I guess that's not a possibility." Sam scuffed a heel into the gravel. "Is it?"

Ashlyn leveled a perfunctory gaze on him, making Sam wish he'd never been born with a voice to get him in trouble.

"I don't think I want to ride this emotional Tilt-A-Whirl anymore. One day, you're kissing me, the next you're yelling at me."

"I didn't yell."

"Well, you weren't exactly whispering terms of endearment, either."

"Listen," he said, extending a hand. "What do you say we call a truce, eat dinner with the kid, relax a little."

She narrowed her eyes at him, violet standing out more than the other shades. He realized that the purplish color meant suspicion as far as Ashlyn was concerned.

"No real-life conversation?" she asked.

He shook his head. "I promise."

They held each other's gazes, the moment stretching out like the length of a rainbow, drawing Sam to Ashlyn, to her light, her warmth.

"Hey, you two," called Tag.

He stood on the porch, a snapshot clutched in his good hand, his nub planted on a hip, looking as flustered as Sam himself probably did when he was vexed. Had he been around Tag enough for the kid to catch on to his habits?

"Hey, what?" Sam said.

He felt Ashlyn shift next to him, and he moved closer in response.

"Time to eat. I've got everything on plates. With *cold slawn* for Miss Spencer."

"Appreciate it, Tag," Sam said, absently looping his arm around Ashlyn's back to lead her inside.

He heard her intake of breath, felt her relax under his hand, and he was reminded of last night once again.

Damn, what he'd give for a replay.

When they climbed the stairs to the porch, Ashlyn rubbed against him—just for an innocent second— her shoulder against the top of his arm. Sam stifled a shudder of need.

Tag held out the picture. "See, sir? From the fishing trip."

The kid grabbed the snapshot back before Sam could really see it, as if it were the most precious jewel in creation. But Sam had caught a blur of himself and Ashlyn, paired together as if it were natural, as if they were a couple.

Tag said, "I never had a family photo before. Not even of my parents. They were gonna give me away, so why give me a picture, huh?"

Sam reached out to Tag, taking him by his nubby little hand. "I can't imagine anyone ever giving you away again, kid."

"Really?" Tag grinned from ear to ear.

"Really." Something inside Sam broke open as he caught Ashlyn's tear-gleamed eyes.

He straightened to his full height, nodding toward

the door. "Now, scram inside. There's food to be eaten."

Tag backed up, banged into the door, grinned again, and entered the house with nary a complaint.

Ashlyn gave him a playful shove. "You old softy," she whispered, standing on tiptoe to kiss his cheek.

His skin buzzed from the contact, a million tiny bubbles all competing for the recent memory of her touch.

As she crossed his threshold, he thought she didn't look half bad walking into his future.

This time, as he followed, he left the ghosts outside.

After the hearty dinner of *cold slawn,* Ashlyn didn't know if she could take much more of this unspoken tension between her and Sam.

She sat next to him in the Bronco as they headed toward Kane Lane, toward her house. They'd eaten the food in relative peace, laughing at Tag's silly jokes, appreciating his energy for life. Then they'd taken him back to the Reno Center for the night.

As Sam cruised by Locksley Field, Ashlyn caught sight of Meg and Nick's house against the gentian-blue sky.

"Have you ever noticed anything...I don't know...*off* about the Cassidys' house?" she asked softly, almost hating to break their stretch of peace.

Sam's khaki shirt rustled against his skin as he shrugged. "'Off'? What do you mean? Like..."

"Like that magnolia smell?"

Sam chuckled. "Oh, that. Just Valentine Thornton's old furniture and clothing, I suppose."

"You don't think…"

"What, that it's Valentine's spirit?" Sam peered at her out of the corner of his eye. "Now you're sounding like Meg."

"Oh. So the big man doesn't believe in scary stuff, does he?"

"I don't believe there's a man in the moon, either."

With a heavy heart, Ashlyn realized that Sam didn't believe in much.

The old drive-in loomed ahead, and she thought about a work of art she'd created in the car grave-yard, in the rusted Ford. Something she'd never shared with anyone.

Wouldn't it be incredible if she could get Sam to see that man in the moon?

She put a hand on Sam's arm. "Let's stop at the drive-in."

"What?" He actually slowed the car, looked at her as if she'd gone ten kinds of loony.

"I want to show you something."

He lifted an eyebrow, a slow smile spreading over his mouth.

Ashlyn grinned. "Don't get excited, Big Bad Wolf. Can you indulge me for a minute?"

Sam turned up his palm, surrendering. He pulled alongside the deserted, silver-washed road, cut the engine and alighted the Bronco.

Ashlyn sat in her seat, waiting for him to open her door.

Did girls still do that? Expect their dates—or whatevers—to be gentlemen? Ashlyn hadn't gone on a date of her own choice since college, when she'd seen a few boys who'd caught her slight fancy.

But she'd never had enough interest in them beyond dinner and a movie.

She was a bit curious to find out what happened after the formal part, when a man and a woman found themselves alone and hungry for each other.

Maybe she could find out what happened with Sam Reno's help.

He pulled open the car door, and Ashlyn took his hand to jump out, wondering if Sam was interested enough to go beyond the kissing stage. The thought left her without breath to speak.

As they walked toward the drive-in, he didn't let go of her hand. She took the opportunity to feel his skin, the masculine strength of his calluses, the urgency of his grip.

"Head toward the Ford, okay?" she said, almost gasping from trying to keep up with his long strides.

His voice floated on the night-warmed, late-Spring air. "I'm still not sure I want to be doing this."

They entered the drive-in's fence, a gate groaning behind them on its hinges. The snack stand stood empty, ringing with the memory of bustling teenagers buying popcorn and sodas.

Sam led her through the maze of abandoned rocking horses, wheelbarrows, bicycles and the like. Finally, they came to the convertible.

Suddenly, Ashlyn wasn't so sure she wanted to be doing this, exhibiting a private side of herself. She hadn't shown her motor-inspired artwork to anyone before him, hadn't taken the chance that someone would criticize it and break her heart.

What the heck, she told herself. Making him understand the magic you see in everyday life is far more important than your artistic confidence.

She lightly pushed him into the car's long front seat, not that there was any choice. The only back seat doubled as a trunk, hardly inspiring her to huddle with Sam there.

Ashlyn scooted inside, as well, watching Sam expectantly as the moon iced over him through the open roof.

"Well?" he asked.

"Don't be a grouch. Just take a gander."

Sam looked around the car, seemingly unimpressed. Then, as his gaze lowered to the steering wheel, a slight smile lit over his face. "I'll be damned," he said.

Months ago, an idea had come to her while she'd philosophized in this car. She'd experimented with the steering wheel, shaping it into a half-sphere face with additional metals, tweaking the edges to resemble graceful arms and legs—people escaping earth to run to the man in the moon, to ask him for wisdom.

She laughed to cover her anticipation. "Whenever I don't want to be home, I come out here to get away from it all, I guess. I think I came up with this sculpture after I'd declined to go to Italy."

"To study art there," Sam said.

When she shot a wondering glance at him, Sam lifted his hand, his fingers waving dismissively. "Rachel and Meg told me."

"Oh." So he'd been talking about her with other people? The thought warmed her, gave her hopes that shouldn't have been lingering in her soul.

But, still… Was Sam interested in her?

He leaned back in the seat, crossing his arms over his chest in a casual manner. He nodded at the steering wheel sculpture. "I guess I can see that man in the moon now." He turned to her. "You're really pretty good at this art stuff."

Ashlyn felt herself blush. "I could be better. With training, with more inspiration." With more confidence.

He reached out to touch her necklace, skimming against the skin of her chest in the process. Her stomach flip-flopped, the sensation flooding her lower regions as a consequence.

"What inspired *this?*" he asked, his mouth curved in that side-smile.

She didn't want to answer his question because she couldn't bear to think about anything other than the heat from his touch, the quivers that had started massaging her skin.

She decided to answer simply. "A childhood memory."

"Not that I know much about art and all, but you have a lot of broken circles in your work, Ashlyn." Sam thumbed toward the wheel. "Even your moon doesn't connect."

"You noticed." Nobody had before, not even best friends who'd seen the rest of her sculptures and jewelry.

"What's going on inside your head?" he whispered, his hand lingering on her chest.

"A wasteland of useless ideas," she said softly.

They both just sat in that front seat, unwilling to move, to break the moment. Ashlyn wondered if he could feel her heart ramming her chest with anticipation.

He gazed into her eyes, using his other fingers to coax back a short lock of hair that had covered her forehead. "I'd better get you home," he said.

"I don't feel like going home just yet."

She realized how much the words resembled an invitation of sorts. Heck, why hadn't she just blurted out that she wanted him to kiss her again?

Something in his eyes flared to life, and his fingers traveled down from her necklace to ease over her breast. Ashlyn closed her eyes as their lips connected again, completing her circles.

His mouth covered hers completely, brushing, probing, making her want to taste more of him. His woodsy scent crashed through her senses, a combination of fallen leaves and fresh air.

He settled over her soul like a blanket of springtime, covering her with a layer of warmth and security. Ashlyn wished they could stay locked in this car forever, away from a world of family war zones.

She nuzzled her nose against his cheek, drawing away from his lips. As she leaned against him, his chest heaved for breath, floating her up and down in the wake of his kiss.

Breathlessly she said, "Did you ever take a girl to the movies here?"

Sam chuckled, the sound reverberating through Ashlyn. His laugh was the most intimate moment her body had ever experienced. She'd always wondered what lying against a man would feel like, with her spooned to his back or him curved into hers.

She knew now. It was like having Sam be a part of her, his laughter traveling through her body as if they were joined together.

But she was getting ahead of herself. She turned

onto her back, nestling onto the bulk of his chest, feeling his badge ridging into her hair like cold, blunt fingers. The stars blinked back at her from the endless sky, hardly believing that Sam Reno and Ashlyn Spencer were here by themselves, cozy as two drive-in-hopeful teens.

After he'd finished laughing, Sam slid his hands over her stomach, his fingers slipping under her light sweater to trace the edges of her belly button. Hot tremors sizzled in her stomach, spreading fire all over.

His breath stirred the hair by her ear as he whispered, "I guess I visited this place a few times too many."

"With who?" Her voice trembled ever so slightly while she fought for calm.

"I don't know. I went steady with a couple girls. Tina Goodwin, Stephanie Burks, Jo Ann Walters—"

The last name made her remember the teenage Sam giving Jo Ann a bunch of flowers. "What a list, Romeo."

Sam tickled her, causing Ashlyn to start and laugh, grabbing his hands. Eternity passed as she awaited his next move. Their breathing paced each other's, a tempo of uneven gasps for air. He ran his palms upward to cup her breasts, his fingers splaying over their fullness, his thumbs exploring the hardened tips. It was all she could do to keep her cool, to steady her heartbeat.

He traced one hand toward her jawline, dragging it over the tender center of her neck as it arched under his touch. He tilted her face toward him, their lips melding together once more, their breath in-

creasing in time until—in an explosive instant—
Ashlyn turned over, fitting the length of her body
against his.

The front seat cramped their long legs, but Ashlyn
didn't mind the lack of space. As she rubbed against
him, she could feel the bulge under his jeans—firm,
hot and ready.

He cupped her rear end, encouraging her to press
against him harder. The silent suggestion spurred a
deeper kiss, his tongue sliding in to stroke hers,
marking a rhythm to their lazy, front-seat dance.

Ashlyn could almost imagine the drive-in speak-
ers hanging on the Ford's missing window, broad-
casting lines from a sci-fi movie or playing the slow
notes of a summer-night love song. She felt alive,
here in a forbidden place with a forbidden man.
And, most important, she felt secure, encased by the
sleek, hard muscles of his arms.

Ashlyn began to unbutton his shirt, and Sam
groaned beneath her busy fingers. She traced her
hands inside the material, feeling warm skin covered
by a slight down of hair. Her breasts pushed against
his ribs, exciting her further.

"Dammit, Ashlyn," he muttered, hesitating, his
hands in the air, as she bent over to sketch her lips
over his broad chest, his peaked nipples.

As she looked up at him, he shut his eyes, head
averted to the side.

She was losing him.

Even as Ashlyn tried to ignore the thought, a sob
gathered in her throat, raging to chase away the pain
of his past. She wanted to tap his memories on their
shoulders and cut in for the rest of Sam's life. Heck,

she would've even settled for the next hour, she thought with a touch of ruefulness.

Ashlyn pulled up, adjusting her light sweater over her stomach even as she straddled his body. His arousal still beat beneath the center of her legs, causing her to back off of him.

He opened his eyes, pushed up to balance on one forearm, his other hand reaching for her. "Don't go," he said softly.

Sam Reno, resting under the moonlight.

Ashlyn remembered his romantic, teenage figure bursting into her life at the age of seven, when she'd still been young enough to fantasize safely.

However, Jo Ann Walters was in his past, but the ghost he was still courting—the wife who'd died so tragically—seemed as though it would keep Ashlyn and Sam apart forever.

As she watched the fullness of his lower lip and the enticing sight of his open shirt, showcasing a ridged belly, she came a whisper away from cozying back into his embrace. Yet she couldn't do it.

Her voice wavered. "You know she's always going to be right next to you, Sam."

He watched her, something akin to regret in his dead gaze. His hand lowered, and he clutched it to his side.

He hadn't even asked who "she" was.

Ashlyn didn't know what to say, knew only that she needed to be away from him and his past.

With as much rapid dignity as she could muster, she slid out of the car, missing his heat as she walked toward the gates, toward the path that led back to the Spencer mansion.

He didn't call her back, and Ashlyn couldn't say she was surprised.

Chapter Eleven

Last night's sexual electricity burned Ashlyn with memories of Sam's long, muscled body. She knew she needed to see him again. And it wasn't because she wanted him with every curious pulse of her heart.

It was because of a factory accident. A real one, this time.

She pulled in to his gravel driveway, the sound of rubber against stone crushing her nerves. A lone lamp shone through the lace curtains, making her wonder if Sam was burning the midnight oil, trying to get her father in trouble.

Sam had paid a tense visit to the Spenco office today, firing bullet-quick questions at Horatio Spencer, accusing him of using faulty machinery. She'd heard her father discussing the matter on the phone with a lawyer.

When he'd seen her in the hallway outside his office, he'd clamped shut his mouth. No shock there. Her father left all the business to Chad, the chosen one.

Just another symptom of second place, she supposed.

Now, Ashlyn climbed the steps leading to Sam's front porch. Exhaling, her stomach jittered with tiny trembles, remnants of last night's caresses, phantom trails left by Sam's fingertips over her skin.

She knocked on his door.

Moments passed before Sam answered, warily coaxing the wood open a crack, peering through with one jaded eye. He didn't say anything.

She decided to not mince words, thinking that her diced feelings from last night sported enough damage. "I think we need to talk."

The door creaked open, revealing the long length of Sam, dressed in his signature jeans and lawman's shirt. Both had faded since she'd officially met him, but Sam, himself, hadn't relaxed quite as much. He seemed just as inflexible as the day he'd hauled her to the sheriff's office for trespassing on Emma Trainor's property.

He leaned a broad shoulder against the door frame. Upon a closer look, she realized that what she'd seen in his eyes wasn't a lack of emotion as much as an excess of it.

Sadness, loss filled his gaze.

"What do we have to say to each other?" he asked.

She wondered what was running through his mind. Memories of his father's death? His mother's pain?

"Sam, you really don't think my family killed your father, do you?"

His gaze ran over her, as if a flash of the previous evening's kisses had assaulted him. "Unfortunately, the Spencers have a history when it comes to destroying people. I wouldn't put anything past your father."

"I thought you knew better, Sam." She shook her head. "Today's accident didn't even involve machinery. Three addle-brained workers were fooling around on the assembly line, trying to scare each other by jabbing rivet guns at their ribs. A gun went off, and it injured one of them. Now I know that this can't bring back good memories for you, but today had nothing to do with your father."

"Are you on the goodwill committee for Spenco?"

He seemed so lifeless, so...dead inside.

She mirrored his stance, folding her arms. "Don't make this into something it isn't. I know you wear a badge, and that means you need to find the truth. Justice. But can't you take my word?"

He looked past her, avoiding her gaze.

She ignored the slight. Thoughts of Charlie Reno's death rushed her. He'd allegedly been caught in a storm of cogs and teeth while attempting to shut down a machine as it threatened another worker. Investigators had said that he'd ultimately caused the entire structure to crash down onto the ten other employees.

Sam looked up again. Embers were kindling in the hazel of his eyes. "I wanted your father to know that I'm watching every move. Greed's going to get the better of him, Ashlyn. I feel it in my bones, just like I knew that the meth cooker in D.C., was up to no good.''

Once again, the comparison stung. As she met his gaze, Ashlyn wished she, herself, had the power to make him feel a spark again. "Then we're at loggerheads, Sam. You think my dad is guilty. I want to prove to you that he isn't.''

She waited a beat. Then he stepped aside, opening the door wider to allow her access into his home.

"You know,'' she said, "it's not like this is Washington, D.C., where you have to interrogate everyone who comes to your door.''

He led the way into his family room, open cardboard containers scattered around the floor. "I like to play it safe.''

"No kidding, Sam.'' She pointed at the empty boxes. "You've finally unpacked? Or are you packing up?''

"I'm settling in. When Mr. Martin moved to his new digs in Tennessee, he left a lot of old stuff in the basement. I didn't have a whole lot of my own things to bring from D.C., so I decided to give his belongings the once-over.'' He shrugged, as if none of it mattered.

Loneliness swept over her. Wasn't it typical though? When she and Tag had eaten dinner here last night, he'd still been unpacked. Now that he had a purpose in life—to revisit his father's death—he was willing to move in, to settle.

She hadn't been enough to make him unpack.

He'd already spread various items on the carpet: table linens, books, lamps, knickknacks, records. As she walked farther into the room, she noticed that he'd shined up a gramophone and an old radio, one that domed in the center like the middle of a cathedral roof.

Ashlyn sat next to the gramophone, stroking the bloom of the speaker. "This looks like a seashell. Does it still play records?"

"Yeah. How're you going to prove your father's innocence?"

His patent impatience unnerved her. "Are you a pod person who took over Sam Reno's body?" The body she'd smoothed her mouth over last night?

Sam sighed, huffed the plastic covering off the couch and sat down, forearms on his thighs. "I'm sorry. But... Have you ever wanted something so badly you'd die for it?"

Ashlyn kept her peace but, inside, a maelstrom brewed. Yes, she had. She'd wanted her family's love, Sam's affection.

He continued. "I want the truth, Ashlyn. Can you understand?"

"And you're willing to destroy my father for it. I see."

"I'm not hurting anyone. I'm making things right and maybe even saving a few lives in the future."

She hated that they were avoiding the real reason for their discomfort. Sam obviously regretted being with her last night.

She swallowed, casually lifted up a stack of records. Names like Johnny Mercer, Betty Hutton and Ella Fitzgerald stared back at her, dull and lifeless.

"I guess this is a good time to present my plan to you then," Ashlyn said.

Was it her imagination, or had he edged closer in anticipation?

She forced her chin up, ignoring his need for

something to correct, something to find closure in. "I don't believe my father caused your dad's death, Sam. There are more personal reasons I'm angry with him, but he's not a monster."

Monster. She had to pause, wondering if she'd just lied to Sam. To herself.

Ashlyn continued. "And I want the chance to prove it to you."

Sam leaned back onto the couch, interest evidently lost. His long legs stretched in front of him, his arms cushioning his head as he reclined. Ashlyn thought of the tautness of his stomach, of running her fingernails over the skin to brush through his chest hair.

He said, "This is your offer?"

"I can go where you can't, Sam. And, let's face it. If you thought you had enough reason, you would've already secured a search warrant." She locked gazes with him. "Listen, I'm not out to prove my father's guilt. I intend to show that you're worrying for no good reason."

She softened her voice. "What happened to your dad was tragic. But it was a terrible accident. Only that."

"An accident that could've been prevented. My dad knew that those machines needed to be replaced with a better brand. Your father tried to paint him as a paranoid lunatic, protected by the union. But my dad ended up being right. And dead."

She shivered, wondering when his eyes had cleared from their purgatory-hazel shade to this new tint of green. "You sound an awful lot like Nick when he first came to Kane's Crossing."

His gaze darkened, and he leaned forward again. "What are you planning to do, Ashlyn?"

She traced over the crinkled record package, hating his fervor. "I have access to paperwork, things in my father's office at the factory and at home. And don't look so excited because I know I'm not going to find anything incriminating."

In her mind's eye, Ashlyn felt the rocks crashing downward, breathed in the resulting dust, strangled the scream that grew within her small, seven-year-old body. She was in the cave again, afraid because she'd seen something she wasn't supposed to see. Afraid because, all these years, she hadn't known what it meant.

She was afraid she might know now.

"I'm going to show you the truth," she said. *And I need to know it myself. For my own peace of mind.*

He didn't speak, just stared into space, his eyes alive with a meaningless purpose.

She'd lost him. But she'd be darned if it was forever.

Two days later the sun peeked between gunsmoke clouds as it hovered over the Reno Center's expansive lawns. Young boys and girls played flag football, pieces of blue and red material flying from the belts at their waists as they ran down the grass, their speed as fleeting as childhood itself.

Sam and Ashlyn sat in lawn chairs, watching Tag play running back, tucking the football under his arm to avoid using his nubby hand.

Ashlyn stretched out her slender legs, smoothing a skirt over her thighs. Sam's fingers tingled, wishing they could follow her lead, knowing at the same time it was the world's worst idea.

She adjusted her cat-eyed sunglasses. "Wow. Good thing we decided to meet on neutral ground to compare evidence, Sam. We have to keep a low profile in these spy games."

Though her tone was light, he detected a slight edge. Maybe it was because she was literally spying on her family, even if she thought she was doing it for the right reasons.

Guilt weighed heavily on him. Yeah, maybe he was overreacting to this factory mishap, but all Sam wanted was the truth—and it felt good. It made him strong with purpose, led him out of the dead zone his life had become.

Ashlyn's honeyed scent wafted over to him, reminding Sam that a damned good purpose for living was sitting right next to him.

Ninety-five percent of him just wanted to reach out and hold her again, taking up where they'd left off the other night.

"What have you got?" he asked, ignoring the heat of memory.

She handed him a manila folder. "Old memos, printouts of e-mails and computer files. But if you'll look carefully, you'll see that my father is as clean as a whistle."

"Don't sound too triumphant. Something will show up."

Ashlyn made an exasperated sound. "Stop wallowing in delusions, Sheriff."

Pow. Back to where they'd started, calling each other "Sheriff" and "Miss Spencer." Sam was sorry their situation had deteriorated, especially since his body wanted to go way past formalities.

She seemed so happy to have found nothing incriminating. In a way, he was glad for her, too, but not excessively. Sam knew Horatio Spencer was hiding something rotten in his factory, in his files. It was only a matter of time until they found it.

Ashlyn clapped her hands and yelled encouragement to Tag as the kid ran for a touchdown. "He's pretty good," she said, grinning from ear to ear.

Thoughts of the future assailed him: Ashlyn cheering on her children as they excelled in soccer, gymnastics or even piano playing; Ashlyn tucking a child into bed after laughing with them while reading a picture book; Ashlyn snuggling under the sheets to cuddle with a shape in the bed beside her…

Who was that shape?

He frowned. It wouldn't be him.

He turned his attention to Tag, on his victory dance in the end zone. Poor kid looked like a chicken with its head cut off. Sam guessed he'd have to teach Tag a more dignified way to celebrate.

"Tag can do anything he sets his mind to," said Ashlyn.

Sam felt a smile growing. "You'd never guess he could, what, with the strikes he has against him."

"It's funny how some people consider his challenges to be strikes."

She stared pointedly at him from under her sunglasses, and an aw-gosh heat stole up his neck. "Okay. I didn't mean it that way."

"I know."

She sighed, making Sam aware of how she hid her sadness behind such a cavalier facade. Beneath the ready smile and diamond-bright eyes, there was a lot of pain. For Tag, for her family.

She said, "I almost cried when he said his parents gave him away. How could anyone do that? To any of these children?"

Sam thought of all the kids who'd gotten away from their parents somehow. An old wound tore open in his soul, but he did his best to banish the desolate memory.

He shifted, the manila folder weighing heavily in his lap. "I hate to rush things, but I have to get back to work." He indicated the walkie-talkie on his belt. The fact that it had remained silent for the past half hour didn't help his cause, but he had to distance himself, to empty his thoughts of her once again.

"I get the hint, Sheriff."

"Dammit, would you just call me Sam again?"

He hadn't meant to say it with such frustration, such pent-up anger. "I apologize, but this is ridiculous, Ashlyn. We've got to learn to get along."

"All right, then. All business, Sam. Did you do your research?"

Good, back on civil ground. He was more comfortable here, even though he had a sneaking suspicion that he was using this business as a convenient excuse to push her away, to refuse to get closer to a woman who could break his heart again.

"As you know," he said, "I don't have access to the factory, but I've got some feelers out with some of my former law enforcement connections in D.C. I'm also trying to find some background on old Spenco factory accidents."

"Having any luck?" She smiled, a saccharine gesture.

"Not yet. My time has been crunched by Rachel Shane's latest dilemma."

Ashlyn tilted her head. "What's wrong?"

"You haven't heard?" He wondered why Ashlyn always started acting fidgety whenever they talked about Rachel Shane.

"No. Last I knew, she was on her way to New Orleans to be reunited with her husband."

"Not her husband," Sam said.

Ashlyn's cocked eyebrow rose above the glasses. Damn, he wanted to reach out and smooth it down with his thumb.

"Turns out that it was some guy who'd gotten a hold of Matthew Shane's ID. The schmuck said he found Matthew's wallet on the street. Thought the credit cards would make some fine purchases."

"So he's still missing."

Sam remembered Rachel's tear-choked voice on the phone last night, asking him to look into the matter further. She'd fired her private detective in frustration, and Sam had promised to do his best. He already had another detective in mind if Rachel decided to go that route again.

"Yeah, Matthew's still gone." Sam paused. "You don't like Rachel much, do you?"

Ashlyn seemed taken aback. "Actually, I do. *Everyone* seems to like her."

"She's a bit standoffish because of Matthew but, yeah, fairly likable."

"Pretty, too."

Oh, for land's sakes. "What are you asking, Ashlyn?"

"Nothing." She raised her chin and watched the football game.

He wasn't thinking straight when he reached out to run his fingers through her hair. For a moment she froze, then leaned into him. Why wasn't he removing his hand, taking back his sanity?

"I'm sorry for taking advantage of you the other night," he said, memories of a leg-cramped front seat at the drive-in fogging the windows of his mind.

"You didn't take advantage of anything, you big dolt."

Sam almost raised his arms in pure vexation as he moved away from her. "What are you mad about now?"

"You're apologizing for something good and—" She stopped short.

Sam chanced a look at her. She bit her lip, probably holding back words both of them couldn't handle. He wondered how strongly she felt about him, if she'd come to care about him.

Instinct told him to run, to disappear from his troubles as quickly as possible. But that's what he'd done after his father had died, after Mary had died. He couldn't keep leaving.

As a cloud passed over the sun, Ashlyn's sunglassed gaze settled on his shirt.

"You've shined up your badge."

So he had. It was about time, too. He was sick of the rust, sick of not caring. "If I'm going to be a decent sheriff, I need to look the part."

"That's funny," she said. "I thought you were doing just fine. Has my family's problems given you so much purpose?"

She stopped cold, looking away. "I'm sorry. I'm not trying to sugarcoat your dad's death."

Pain surrounded his heart, throbbing with old

scabs being stretched apart by her statements. He couldn't bring himself to respond.

"Shoot." She stood, folded her lawn chair. "I should just leave before I say something ultimately awful."

Her skirt fluttered in the wind, butterfly's wings ready to take flight. Sam needed to think about his answer, long and hard.

He paused. What the hell could he say? *Would you please stay with me, no matter what happens?*

Should he confess that he wanted her beyond all power? That he couldn't have her for any number of reasons? Especially since he was scared to death Ashlyn would end up hurting him, freezing him for life?

Finally he settled on a response. "I appreciate your help on this matter, Ashlyn."

Mentally, he cursed himself, hating that he couldn't say what really mattered.

She watched him for a moment, her rainbow eyes shielded by the sunglasses. Sam felt so uncomfortable he wanted to join the groundhogs by digging an escape hole.

Ashlyn shook her head. "I'll keep looking for evidence, Sam, but only because…"

Silence, except for the taunts of the football-crazy children.

She sighed. "Never mind."

As she left, Sam would have given anything to know what Ashlyn wanted to say. But in his heart of hearts, he already knew.

He only hoped she hadn't gone and done such a fool thing as getting soft on him. Because he would never be able to return the emotion.

Not with the way he'd blown it in the past.

* * *

Ashlyn Spencer had promised Sam that she would keep looking for evidence. And she had, throughout the night, sneaking past the lone, half-awake factory security detail, searching the mammoth, rust-laced machinery as well as her father's office.

A few years ago, before realizing the extent of her father's apathy toward her, Ashlyn had entertained the notion that her father would put her in charge of one of their businesses—just as he'd done with Chad. Of her own initiative, she'd spent a long summer exploring the factory, working in it, gleaning information from the workers about the running of it, the machinery, the products. Hopefully she could use this knowledge to prove her family's innocence.

Now, after her cursory search, she found nothing incriminating. She'd known all along that she wouldn't.

But then she returned home, awakening early the next morning, waiting until her father had gone to work. She'd tiptoed into his home office, shuttered windows making the room seem cave-dark. She'd riffled through his papers, file cabinets, anything she hadn't investigated thoroughly before.

And she'd found this.

She ran a finger over the golden lettering on the front of the ledger. Accounts it said, the leather cover seeming as innocent as the leaves of a Venus's-flytrap.

Inside it told her everything, echoing Sam's suspicions, confirming her worst fears.

Those niggling thoughts that had been eating

away at her as she'd lay prone in the cave had taken this ledger's form. Part of her hadn't even believed she'd seen anything that day, but part of her knew that what happened in the dark domain hadn't been a dream—or an accident.

Now she knew for certain.

She remembered when, months ago, she used to spend time with the old men rocking in chairs with cigars poised by their mouths, playing checkers amid a slow flurry of gossip on the general store porch. She remembered what old Ikey Ribble had said the day after Nick Cassidy had purchased the factory. *Maybe that new fella will see to some safety at that place. Things ain't been the same there since the first accident.*

Ashlyn had assumed Ikey had been talking about the misfortune that had killed Sam's father. But she'd been wrong.

She opened the book, the old paper cackling with the movement. It was all here in the various entries, written in her father's careful scrawl. Seventeen years ago, the first factory accident occurred, in which a man had been caught in the machinery, paralyzing him. Four months later the ancient machinery was destroyed. New equipment—the same brand—had been purchased for a fortunate pittance. Then, eleven years after that, Sam's father and ten others had died in the big accident that still haunted Kane's Crossing.

She'd read it all, and knew how, after the seventeen-year-old accident, her father ordered the same brand of machinery because he'd cut a sweet deal with the manufacturer. She knew he had his doubts about the safety of that equipment as it aged, because he'd noted it, checked into getting it fixed, too, until it hadn't proven cost-effective. She knew that he'd kept using the machinery in spite of its dangerous record.

Sam needed this information so he could prosecute. The workers needed this information for their safety. But what if this ledger misrepresented the Spencer family?

She needed to hear an explanation from her father before taking the matter to Sam. After all these years, she felt she deserved one.

Sam. Ashlyn's heart expanded with an unknown force, filling her whole. His name was like a warm fire on a cold night, pulling her near, comforting her.

She wanted to help him, wanted to make him forget the pain of his father's senseless death. This ledger would brighten his eyes, because it contained the information necessary to clear Charlie Reno's name.

Her conscience flared. Giving Sam the ledger would also ruin her family. She was backed into a corner. Even so, if she gave Sam the ledger now, would it make him love her?

You know that's not the case. Sam's never going to fall in love with you. Even if you are half over the moon for him.

And it was true. She was so in love with him that it pained her to think about it. It made her want to sing, to paint sun-burst pictures on a cloud, made her want to bury herself in her bedcovers and cry her heart out.

What was she going to do first? Help Sam? Or confront her own father?

Ashlyn slowly tucked the ledger under her arm;

it weighed like the world, dragging her heart down. She couldn't believe her father had done these things, had allowed greed to overwhelm his sense of protecting his workers.

But she knew he'd always been like that.

God, the cave. It all made more sense. All the dreamy images were hardening into rock-pointed shards, stabbing her conscience.

She needed to go back, to see if she'd imagined what she'd seen in the cave when she was seven years old. To find out about the evidence the ledger had dusted off in her own mind. Then, she needed to hear her father tell her—privately—that he was guilty.

Ashlyn walked out of her father's home office, wanting to find the truth for herself *and* Sam.

An hour later, as sunset waited in the wings of the late-afternoon sky, Ashlyn stood by the mouth of the cave. She was trying her best to hide from the Reno Center kids, who were field tripping here near Factory Bluff, climbing on the rocks, poking their heads in and out of the rocky crevices.

She turned her attention back to the yawning cave entrance, hoping Tag hadn't accompanied these children today. Caves were dangerous—she knew firsthand.

Exhaling, she took her first step, clicking on the flashlight she'd brought with her. She'd left the ledger at home, hoping to distance herself from thoughts of her father.

But now she needed proof that the ledger was accurate. And that proof would be found here.

Her necklace pounded against her chest, the

gravel chunk in the middle of the silver half circles drumming like a heartbeat.

It was dark, so dark.

Maybe she should have brought Sam with her.

Daggonit, why couldn't she forget him, especially at a time like this?

She leaned against a cave wall, breathless with mingled fear and memories of Sam's hands cupping her breasts, skimming down her stomach to rub over her skin.

While he was amusing himself with her body, he probably had no intention of ever loving her. He'd probably been as emotionless as the desert-scape stillness of his hazel eyes.

Was she so inadequate that she couldn't get anyone to love her?

Stop being petulant, she told herself, pushing off from the wall, shining the light on the rock and searching for landmarks of memory.

As a seven-year-old, she'd known this cave. She'd had enough time to emboss every crag, every fissure, into her mind. She'd lay prone, her arms pinned to her sides, robbed of breath by the coffin-like dearth of fresh air.

Ashlyn gasped, telling herself that she wasn't a child anymore, that she no longer followed her brother like an affection-starved puppy, that she no longer hid under bleachers and spied on Sam Reno-type football players who kissed cheerleaders.

There, near the maze of fallen rocks.

She played the flashlight's beam over the rubble, feeling claustrophobic.

Get me out of here, Mommy and Daddy.

The place had been cleared out pretty well,

cleaned of the rocks and debris that had littered the ground. Ashlyn moved closer, inspecting the dirt.

Why was she here, anyway? It wasn't like she'd find anything—evidence, machinery, her self-confidence.

A short time later, a glimmer caught her eye. The first thing she thought of was the new shine of Sam's badge. A jolt of affection squeezed her heart.

Then she moved closer, recognizing metal, an object uncovered by a cave inhabitant scrounging for food, perhaps.

She blew on the dirt, uncovering the item.

It was a bolt.

Shrapnel from an explosion that had occurred when she was seven.

A terrible sob ripped out of Ashlyn, and she sank to the ground, once again trapped and lonely.

So lonely.

Chapter Twelve

"Ashlyn!"

Sam's voice, echoing through the darkness, was the only response. He whisked his flashlight over the mouth of the cave, then turned to the little boy next to him.

Lanterns from the other search party members, including his brother Nick, made Tag's dark eyes stand out like deep holes, hollowed out from the skin. The night sky enveloped the child, all but swallowing his small body whole.

"Are you sure she went in one of these caves?" Sam asked, hoping he sounded strong and sure.

Tag nodded, balancing his weight on one foot then the other. "Yes, sir. This afternoon, me and some friends were playing hide-and-go-seek over yonder when I saw her. Teacher said that I had to stay with them though. Miss Spencer never came out the whole time. We came to get you when she didn't show up for art tonight…''

Sam reached out to lay a hand on Tag's black hair. The child stilled under his touch.

He addressed the search party. ''There are a few openings around here. Why don't we partner up and keep in contact with the walkie-talkies?''

The men agreed, splitting up. Sam scanned the crowd, keeping a mental tally of who was with whom. He tried not to grimace when he noted the absence of Ashlyn's own father.

Deputy Joanson whipped the communication unit out of his belt, positioning it closer to his mouth. ''Testing, testing.''

Sam didn't have the patience or humor to chastise the man. After all, he was trying to help. Hell, they'd all been trying for two hours, until Tag had identified the right set of caves.

He was doing his best not to think of Ashlyn trapped in there, injured. Or worse.

Sam cursed under his breath. He wasn't able to stop his dead wife's fate, hadn't been able to keep her out of the car, or stop the driver who'd killed her. But he damned sure could help Ashlyn.

He tried not to choke on his words. ''Let's rendezvous in one hour. That's nine o'clock, gentlemen. Nick, can you stay out here with Tag and be our point guy?''

Nick nodded. The brothers traded a glance fraught with meaning. Sam knew that Nick was fully aware of his misguided fascination with Ashlyn Spencer, and he knew Sam was tying himself in worried knots over her disappearance.

When the men had dispersed, Sam found himself alone. He led Tag to Nick's open arms.

"I'll take this cave since Tag thinks it's my best shot."

"Be careful, Sam." Nick's gaze reflected his concern.

Tag gave him one last hug. "Don't get lost, too," he said.

At first, Sam didn't know what to do with this kid in his arms. His hands hovered in the air, and he saw how Nick averted his gaze. Gradually, Sam found the strength to plant his palms on Tag's back, soothing the child.

It felt so right, having Tag near him. Sam wondered if the emotion would sustain itself or be destroyed with the speed of a hit-and-run smash.

"I'll be back, kid. And don't worry. I'll keep in touch. Nick, if I'm not here at nine, come in after me."

"Will do."

They shook hands. "Good luck, big brother," said Nick, meeting Sam's eyes.

With that, Sam stepped into the cave, darkness erasing him. He called Ashlyn's name again, hoping she'd answer, despairing when she didn't.

What had she been thinking? Anyone with half a load of common sense knew better than to go exploring by themselves. Tag said that she hadn't even been carrying anything more than a flashlight.

Something wasn't right, and he knew it. Ashlyn never missed her appointments with Tag.

Don't leave me, he thought.

Of course, he'd made that particular request another night, when she'd left him high and dry in the front seat of that drive-in Ford, but this was far more serious. He'd had a second chance that time, but he wasn't so sure he'd have one now.

And, dammit all, he wanted a second chance. Needed it.

What would life be like without Ashlyn? The question stunned him senseless. As he played the flashlight's beam over dark walls, beaded with moisture, he realized that he couldn't imagine his existence devoid of her sunshine, her sweetheart smile.

He had to find her. Facing a stretch of days, dark as a sky without her stars, was unthinkable. But what if he *did* find her? What would he do then?

"Ashlyn!"

Again, his voice bounced off the cold walls. Up ahead he could see a fork in his path.

"Dammit," he said, with more force than necessary.

Soft words floated on the air. "Is that you, Sam?"

He felt as if he'd found a buried treasure. "Ashlyn?"

"To the left," she said, her voice hardly reflecting his own relief.

Flashlight beam leading the way, he took the appropriate path, noticing the rubble that littered the ground. The light played over Ashlyn, who was blocking her eyes with a dirtied hand.

"My God." Sam dropped to a knee, enfolding her in his arms as his heart raced with the speed of his breath.

She felt stiff, not at all as she had at the abandoned drive-in. He backed away, still embracing her, tilting her chin up with a finger.

"What happened?" he asked.

Her eyes had gone the color of dark ash, the shade of a fire gone out. They were ringed by red half circles.

"Nothing," she said.

"Don't say 'nothing,' Ashlyn. We've got men looking for you in other parts of this cave."

"Sorry," she whispered, her lips trembling.

"Oh, sweetheart, it's fine. It's all right." He pulled her head to his chest, threading his fingers through her soft, sandy hair. "I'm going to get on the walkie-talkie to call off the search."

He reached for it, but Ashlyn's hand clamped over his wrist.

"Just wait. Please."

"What's wrong, Ash?" he whispered into her hair, smelling remnants of her honey-almond sweetness.

She paused, gathering herself. "I—I don't want to go out just yet."

He noticed that one of her hands was clenched, as if holding on to something. "All right. We'll stay here as long as you need to, but I have to tell everyone to go home."

"I won't take long."

He told himself to shut up, to wait out her hesitations with patience.

Damn, it felt good to have her in his arms again. Her breasts crushed against his chest, and he could feel her heart beating through his own skin. As he waited for her to settle her tears, he stroked her cheek, brushing his lips against the softness of her brow.

She tilted up her head, seeking his lips on a sob. A salty sadness coated her mouth as she opened herself to him. They pressed against each other, demanding the intimacy they'd found under the stars at the drive-in.

When had he come to care so deeply about her? Had it been a sneaky thing, hiding in corners, permeating him in his most unsuspecting moments?

She broke away, hiccuping.

He laughed a little, hardly surprised. Part of the reason he felt close to Ashlyn was because she made him smile on the inside. He hadn't felt that way in years and years.

With a start, he realized that his protective shield hadn't gone up; it hadn't stopped him from kissing Ashlyn, hadn't intruded on his thoughts to rack him with guilt.

He smoothed his lips over Ashlyn's forehead. "You scared me to death, you know."

"I didn't mean to."

"Of course you didn't. But it would make me feel a hell of a lot better to get you out of here. You're not hurt, right?"

She cracked a smile, but it didn't reveal any happiness. "Not physically."

"Can you tell me what you were thinking when you came into the cave? And was there a reason you aren't too keen on leaving?"

Ashlyn leaned back, breaking their hold on each other. She sought his hand, and he held it.

"Let me tell you a little story, Sam. Then you can ask your questions."

She'd lost track of time in the cave, sucked into a sort of time warp, dragging her back to her childhood.

When she'd heard Sam's voice, her heart had stuttered, almost wishing he hadn't found her. But the expression on his face had given her hope—and despair.

His eyes, lit by the orange afterglow of the flashlight, had shone with what seemed to be a brew of panic and joy. Nobody had ever looked at her that way in her life. Did she deserve it?

Did he actually care about her?

Well, he wouldn't after she lied to him. And that's what she would do for now—conceal that she had found evidence, then talk to her father, hear his side of the story before she turned over the ledger.

She'd spent her entire life making this decision necessary. Her family deserved the opportunity to correct their mistakes, to tell her the truth. After all, she desperately needed their love, their respect. And she was about to earn it.

When she talked with her father, she was certain he'd tell her the truth, would see the error of his ways. Maybe, then, they could begin healing their familial wounds, become a normal group of people who loved each other above all else.

But, right now, the man she had fallen in love with should be given some explanation.

Sam waited patiently, running his thumb over the inside of her index finger. Ashlyn shivered, her breasts pebbling at his touch.

"Remember when you were seven? How the world was all about playing with your friends and dreaming of being a ballerina or cowboy?"

He nodded, a slight smile on his lips. "I prefer to stay away from thoughts of me in a tutu."

She laughed, a threat of tears lurking under the

effort. "Me, too, Sam. Anyway, I knew that I was the 'late baby' in my family, that Chad would always be the number one child. They never planned to have me, and I was always like wisdom teeth. There, but hardly necessary.

"But it was just a feeling." She let go of Sam's hand and waved it in front of her face, as if chasing off unwanted thoughts.

She tightened her other hand around the bolt she'd found on the cave floor. "I'm off track here."

"It's all right," Sam said.

Memories crashed over her, almost blacking out her thoughts. She'd all but forgotten about the cave's details, but now they were as vivid in her mind as they were in reality.

"It was just before the Fourth of July. Father had been incredibly stressed out because of something happening at work." Something Ashlyn now knew to be the first factory accident, but she kept this information to herself. "Rumor had it that they were going to be testing some fireworks for Independence Day on Factory Bluff. They were warning people to stay away. The factory had even been shut down, and we both know what a panic *that* causes."

Sam slanted her a sorry grin.

She tried to smile, too, but failed. "Chad and his friends, you know Sonny Jenks and Junior Crabbe…"

At Sam's stoic nod she continued. "They all decided to watch those fireworks. Now, at that age, Chad was like a god to me. Seven years older than I was. I thought he knew it all. He'd always try to shoo me off when I'd follow him to the general store for sodas, or when he'd round up his friends to play baseball at the school. I knew better than to follow him up to Factory Bluff that day, but I did it. I really wanted to see the caves, and I knew I could explore as well as any boy could.''

''You never show that sort of initiative,'' Sam said wryly, watching her with what might have been amusement or admiration.

He lifted up her hand to kiss her knuckles, making her feel covered by rock-heavy guilt.

She tried another grin. ''So, when we got up here, we waited. And waited. Nothing was happening so, like typical kids, we got a bit bored. Chad and the boys started exploring the caves, and, when they split up, I followed him into this entrance.''

The moment froze in her mind. Chad, dwarfed by looming cave walls splattered with shafts of afternoon light. Chad, humbled by piles of what looked like factory machinery, the equipment glimmering in the muted darkness like monster jaws.

When they'd heard the men in hard hats coming through to charge the explosives, they'd both hidden in separate places, close enough to see each other sticking out their tongues, exchanging big brother/little sister faces.

Then the men had left, but Chad and Ashlyn hadn't.

They'd had no idea that Horatio Spencer had ordered the machinery—the tools that had seriously wounded a worker even before Sam's father worked there—destroyed because he didn't want the officials to see how dilapidated the equipment had grown.

Ashlyn hadn't known it then, but she'd figured it out in the meantime, thanks to the ledger.

Sam cocked an eyebrow. "I think I remember hearing about this in the paper a long time ago. That was you in the cave-in, wasn't it?"

"Yeah." She looked away, hating that she'd omitted much of the story. The machinery bolt she held felt as heavy as a world of its own—one populated by betrayal and watered by a little girl's tears.

"I'd completely forgotten about that. Ash, you were lucky to survive."

He seemed so sincere, so affected by the news that she wanted to stay in the cave forever to avoid asking her father about the truth.

"I need to explain the next part to you, so you'll..." *So you'll understand the reason I'm not giving you the factory information right this moment. So you'll forgive me for wanting to talk with my father first.*

"I'm listening," he said.

She couldn't ask for more than that. An explosion rocked her memory. "It all happened in the blink of a cat's eye, the rumble of rocks, the crunch of stone blocking me and Chad in the cave. Then there was this total darkness. I could hear someone crying. It might have been me. All I knew was that Chad was on the other side of this wall of granite, and I couldn't see him. I couldn't even move, with the rocks leaning on me. The only thing I could do was scream."

Her pulse rumbled, blood tumbling over itself in her veins. "The other kids got out on their own, and they ran for help. Everyone was safe except me and my brother. About an hour after the cave-in, I could hear my parents' voices outside, shouting. My mother cried and yelled at the county emergency workers. As the men tried to get us out, they talked pretty loudly. They were saying awful things, about how, if they tried to get either Chad or me out, there'd be more of a cave-in.''

''I wonder if it was caused by those fireworks,'' Sam said, his low voice as soothing as a midnight promise. ''At least everything turned out all right in the end.''

How pitiful did she appear right now? Was she bug-eyed with terror? Her insides certainly felt that way.

''Yes, luckily it did turn out fine.'' She paused, almost unable to admit to the next part. ''Next thing I knew, I heard the stones being removed from Chad's side, rocks shifting around on mine. They were getting him out.''

Sam narrowed his eyes. ''But you said—''

''I know. They took the chance that my side would cave in.'' Shame and anger blinded her as she closed her eyes, feeling the tears build up.

''Oh, damn. Damn, Ash. Those idiots.''

He pulled her close again, but she pushed against him, backing away to look in his eyes. ''They needed to make a choice, Sam, I just didn't happen to be the one. At least the workers managed to get me out before any damage was done.''

''But there was damage,'' Sam said.

Yes, she'd known for certain that she was second best to Chad. Her parents had even bet her life on that.

''My family wouldn't even look me straight in the eye when the emergency crew brought me out. I remember my mom crying, her back turned to me.

My father just hugged Chad. Then, when the newspaper reporters came, they included me in that hug.''

"They love you, surely you know that." Sam tilted up her chin with a finger. "There are people who actually care about you, Ashlyn Spencer."

His voice was deep, giving more meaning to the words than first met the ear. Ashlyn wondered if Sam cared, if he could ever love her.

Taking a deep breath, she stood, shaking, brushing dirt from her pants. "You know the rest, Sheriff Sam. I made a habit out of punishing my parents for their decision, and they accepted it, knowing what they did deserved penance. My mother decided to numb herself with painkillers, and my father wouldn't say boo to me about my past antics. We're slightly dysfunctional, in case you hadn't caught on."

After a moment, heavy with her heartbeats, Sam stood, as well, reaching out a hand for her. "Let's get out of the darkness."

"Listen, Sam." She grabbed his fingers, threading them through hers. "I may not have the world's most perfect family, but I still want their love. Does that make any sense?"

He just watched her, shaded by the dim flashlight, making Ashlyn wonder if he knew what she wasn't telling him. That she had evidence enough to put his father's memory to rest, enough to put his soul at ease.

"I understand," he said, his voice flat.

He wouldn't be so compassionate if he knew she could make sense out of his father's death with the ledger's information.

She tried to laugh, to ease her conscience. "Just

think. I experienced a cave-in, and all I got was this lousy piece of rock.''

She flicked at her necklace, the silver half circles humming around the gravel she'd clung to during her endless rescue. She could almost feel the edges cutting into her little-girl palm while she listened to the rescue workers saving Chad, wondering if they were ever going to get to her.

Sam watched her, his eyes filled with something she couldn't identify, something she'd never encountered in all her life. Then he stepped nearer, and she gasped.

He fingered her necklace. As he reached behind her, unhooking the clasp, she felt his warm breath on her skin, felt his chest pressing against hers. The charm's heaviness disappeared as he pulled it away, leaving a lightness she had no right to feel.

Even if he'd removed her burden, the guilt remained.

Without a word, he balled his fist over the jewelry, then stuffed it into his pocket.

"Let's go home," he said.

Ashlyn tightened her grip on the bolt she'd procured in the cave, unable to let it go.

Sam wrapped the wool blanket around Ashlyn, skimming her damp hair away from a bath-warmed cheek.

Huddled against his family-room couch, half-filled containers surrounding her, she wore his old boxers and one of his white, long-sleeved shirts, the scent of Ivory soap and her own brand of sunshine-sweetness permeating the material. As he closed the blanket, he caught a glimpse of her breasts, hardened to darkened peaks.

He swallowed away the lump in his throat. "Can I get you anything?"

"Not right now," she said, rubbing her chin against the wool. Her eyes still held a faraway darkness, unreachable, unrelenting.

Sam shoved his hands into his jeans' pockets, and he sucked in a sharp breath. Something had pricked his finger.

He was about to pluck out the offending object, then he remembered what it was. Ashlyn's necklace—her albatross, with its sharp, incomplete circles. It was a powerful, humbling feeling to hold her pain in his hand.

Just about everything made sense to him. Well, almost everything. Sam still had questions about the holes in her story, but now wasn't the time to ask.

Instead, he racked his own brain for answers. Why had she told him such an obviously humiliating story? And why had she added that bit about needing her family's love?

It all meshed with the uncharacteristic haunting in her gaze, the luminous hints of trouble warped into raven-winged shadows.

She was hiding something from him. He just didn't know what.

Sam shrugged, not knowing what else to do with himself in the face of Ashlyn's silence. "I guess I'll leave you be now. If you want, that is."

Ashlyn peeked up at him with those misty eyes, her lashes a dark fringe emphasizing her quietude. "Could you stay? I mean, your house is still sort of creepy with these boxes staring at me."

"Hey, I made great progress last night with my unpacking." He gestured around the room, at the haphazardly stocked bookshelves and cluttered tables, then laughed. "Should I call an interior decorator?"

She hadn't even cracked a grin. "How about we listen to some music? Or not. I don't know…can't you just sit down and relax? You're making me nervous."

Suddenly, Sam felt like a big lump of male ineptitude—insensitive, unwieldy, graceless as a mound of clay.

He held up a finger to her, as if to say, "Wait, here's an idea." In the next ten minutes he built a fire that lent some personality to the room, not to mention warmth and light. Then he fit a record onto the ancient gramophone that Ashlyn had smiled at the other day. Maybe this would cheer her.

Sam wound up the crank and stepped back as the fire crackled in time to the muted needle thumps.

The moan of a clarinet slithered into their midst, followed by the husky warble of a woman's voice. He imagined the singer stepping up to an oversize microphone, backed by a big band packed with a brass section and tuxedoed musicians.

The record breathed images of thigh-high stockings adorning a woman's legs, of jasmine floating on a balmy breeze, of a curl of cigarette smoke undulating in time to the clarinet's hum.

As Sam turned back to Ashlyn, he stopped, her smile sending shock waves through him. It was pathetic how dumb-shucks happy he felt at having succeeded at pleasing her.

"It's one of Mr. Martin's old records," he explained unnecessarily. "There's a grip of them in the basement."

He approached the couch, his pulse pounding a little harder when Ashlyn scooted over as if in reaction to his proximity.

"I love it," she said, the "L" word echoing loudly in the aftermath.

Sam cleared his throat. "What's she singing about? Stormy weather? Hard times?" He laughed. "Appropriate."

The woman's song continued, sounding tinny and hollow with the record's age.

He stood in front of Ashlyn, hesitating, almost afraid of what would happen if he took a seat so close to her.

"Come here, Sam," she said, her voice as low and melodic as the thrum of a bass string.

The blood in his veins beat in time to that bass, plucked by the invitation in her gaze, the gape of the blanket. Her skin glowed in the firelight, pulsing with warmth and flicker.

It seemed like years before he sat, years before anyone spoke.

"Don't look so scared," she said.

"Scared?" Dammit, he hadn't meant for his voice to come out all scattered, parched and confused as autumn leaves in the wind.

She moved closer to him, and Sam felt his head go fuzzy. It'd been so long since he'd been with a woman, he didn't know if he could hold back any longer.

"Ash, you wouldn't come any closer if you knew what was good for you."

She shirked the blanket from her shoulders, revealing the pucker of her breasts against the shirt, the toasty glow of her skin beneath the material.

"I may not know much about making love, Sam." She smiled. "But that doesn't mean I'm not ready for it."

He reached out, thinking that, maybe, he was more than ready himself.

Chapter Thirteen

Sam jerked back his hand once Ashlyn's statement seeped into his better judgment. "Are you—"

"Does it really matter?" Her eyes were no longer that ashy gray. Now they flamed with the colors of a wild Gypsy dance, bright with swirls of need.

"Yeah, it matters. Your first time with a man should be right. Perfect." And Sam knew without a doubt that he was less than perfect.

She tilted her head, hair sticking out, making her seem so damned vulnerable.

"Would you stop making excuses? Listen, Sam, I think I'm old enough to know whether or not a man is right for me."

He expected his defensive shell to harden around him, deflecting her patent longing. It didn't happen.

There was only the laughing tenor of piano notes as they joined the clarinet, the low throb of a trombone sliding toward him, tempting him. Talking him into momentarily falling for Ashlyn Spencer.

She sighed. "You are taking much too long, Sam Reno."

Still, he hesitated, and that must have been all she could stand.

She traced her hand into his hair, making him feel sculpted, created, under the feel of her searching fingers. Next thing he knew, she'd pulled his mouth to hers.

She was so warm, so inviting. Sam found himself responding to her touch, to the friction of his shirt against her skin.

She mumbled against his mouth, butterfly whispers tickling his lips. "I've wanted you forever, Sam."

"Shh," he said, stopping the kiss long enough to place an index finger over her mouth. They were still pressed to each other, their heartbeats echoing through their bodies. "No more confessions."

And yet, as he said it, he couldn't forget tonight's cave revelation. Sam couldn't explain what he was feeling, but he wanted to make Ashlyn feel complete again. Wanted her to know that she was his choice, his number one, even if it was just for tonight.

He purposefully slipped off the couch, resting a knee on the floor, bringing Ashlyn to a kneeling position. His hands spanned her slim waist, his mouth trailing kisses over her stomach.

She braced herself, palms on his shoulders. "Sam..." she whispered.

He recognized her breathiness, the lull of her soft voice. He'd heard it before, in the front seat of the Ford.

He eased his fingertips under her shirt, over her toned stomach, her ribs, under her arms, down her back, all while using his tongue to rim her belly button.

Her muscles quivered, seemingly caught between a nervous laugh and pent-up desire. Ashlyn wriggled against him as he grazed her skin with his teeth playfully.

Then, the next gramophone song settled over the room, muted trumpets set to a slow, sinuous beat.

Sam didn't feel like flirting any longer. Too much blood had pounded into his brain. Too much time had passed since he'd cared for a woman.

As Ashlyn ran her fingernails over the back of his neck, leaving trails of fire, Sam discarded his shirt. He watched the change come over her face—from anticipation to pure need.

He unbuttoned her shirt, slipping his hands underneath the material to worship her breasts, his thumbs circling the hardened nipples.

She swayed beneath his touch, shrugging out of the shirt until it draped over the couch. Sam rose up, taking one breast into his mouth, circling with his tongue in time to Ashlyn's gasps of pleasure.

"Sam, I—"

He looked up, not wanting to hear what she might be feeling. "Don't say anything. You'll never be able to take it back."

A cloud passed over her bright eyes. But as he nuzzled into her neck, he tried to forget it, using his thumb to sketch over the middle of her stomach, over the boxers, into the cleft between her legs.

Ashlyn threw back her head, giving Sam access

to her throat, enticing him to taste her sweetness, to mark her scent in his brain.

When had she become important enough to merit a room in his heart? Was it the first night he'd seen her, stepping out of the darkness cast by Emma Trainor's porch? Or had it been the first time he'd kissed her, right in front of the Spencer mansion's gates?

It hardly seemed to matter now. All Sam knew was that he wanted Ashlyn with every runaway spark in his fool body. All he knew was that he'd almost lost her today, and he might have never had the chance to tell her how much he cared.

As she leaned back onto the couch, he stretched on top of her, jeans straining against his arousal. He settled between her legs, pulsing, on the edge of exploding.

Her breasts were flattened against his chest, soft as summer flowers. Sam paused, stroking hair away from her forehead.

"How can someone be so beautiful?" he asked.

Like him, she was still breathing heavily. "Beautiful? Try another line, Sheriff."

He laughed, kissed her behind the ear, inhaling her scent, feeling her blood flow thudding against his skin. Then he looked at her again, running his gaze over the flush of life on her cheeks, the welcome sparkle that had returned to her colorful eyes. Lips, bruised by his kisses.

"It's not a line, Ash," he said softly.

That shadow crossed her face again, quick as a bird winging across his view of the sun. He wondered what she was still hiding from him.

But the moment passed, and she stirred under him, shifting against his hardness.

Her breath caught, her eyes widened.

She tentatively eased her fingers between them, to the zipper on his jeans. The slow slide buzzed over him, heating the room more than the fire ever could.

As they shucked off the denim, Ashlyn hesitated, then wriggled out of the boxers, as well, leaving her body exposed to his gaze.

As he took a slow look over her, she brought her arms up, covering the vulnerable bareness of her skin.

"No," he said, gently laying a hand over her arms, guiding them away so he had the full benefit of her beauty. "I want to know every inch of you...."

He leaned on his side, his palm traveling the length of her body. She was as slim as the curves of a whirlwind, soft as a breeze whispering through a tree's leaves.

"Thank goodness for a slow hand," she said, voice trembling. She'd leaned back her head on a couch pillow, eyes shut, lashes spread on her flushed cheeks.

In spite of her brave statement, she was really shaking. And as he rested his fingertips on her belly, he could feel the deep quivering just under her skin.

"You're perfect, Ash. I can't believe I'm the first man to appreciate your body. Your soft skin." He circled over her stomach, eliciting a slight gasp from her.

"Your curves."

He sketched his knuckles over her hipbones, the swerve of her waist, the crescent of her breast.

"In my eyes," he said, "you're perfect."

She met his gaze, smiled, bit her lip, closed her eyes.

He traced his fingertips back over her body—over the muscle of her calf, between the lines of her sleek thighs, through the moist parting of her legs. He lingered there, delving into the folds, thumb rubbing against the most sensitive part of her.

When he entered her with his fingers, she sucked in a breath, bringing one hand up to her forehead to fist a thatch of sandy hair. Sam leaned over, joining their lips once more.

Ashlyn grabbed on to him, moving with his rhythm. He withdrew his fingers from her, guiding her hand to grasp his own arousal. He helped her run her palm along his length, making him crazy with the need to fulfill them both.

"Damn," he said, realizing that his condoms were in his bathroom, captivated within the fortress of a medicine cabinet.

"What?" she asked, her breathing erratic.

Protection. That's what he needed. Desperately.

He looked down at her, wishing she wasn't so beautiful, so heartbreakingly innocent.

She laughed a little, letting go of him. "It's me, isn't it? I knew I wasn't doing this right. You probably need a girl with more practice."

He smiled and shook his head. "No, sweetheart. I need condoms. They're in the bedroom's bathroom."

"Of course." She grinned sheepishly. "This is all new to me."

His heart—and the other more demanding parts of his body—ached for her. He wanted to say that this was new to him, too. Not the sex, but something he couldn't define. Something he didn't dare think about.

He lifted Ashlyn into his arms and, with a gasp, she wrapped her legs around him as he made his way to the bedroom. As they came to the entrance, they rested against the wall, kissing feverishly.

They stumbled to the bathroom medicine cabinet. With stunning efficiency, he managed to rescue the condoms and take Ashlyn to the cushion of his bed.

He set her down gently, then smoothed the protective sheath over himself.

She watched Sam, lips parted, backing up to the pillows of his bed. "I shouldn't be nervous, right?"

He settled over her, running a finger across her cheekbone. "I'll take care of you. But are you sure you want this?"

She waited a beat, then reached out, urging him closer, leading him into her slick warmth.

He pressed forward with care, almost losing what he had left of his cool at the sweet pleasure of her tightness. She sucked in a quick breath, making him wait. Then she pressed her palms into his back, heated imprints marking him forever.

"Sam..." Her voice came out on a feverish plea.

She shifted under him and, instinctively, he pushed farther inside of her, knowing all the while that he was in danger of losing himself.

As they moved together, strains of the abandoned gramophone music haunted the air. Their lips joined together, and, all of a sudden, Sam's mind became hers. His body did, too.

Almost his entire being belonged to this woman who writhed beneath him, running her fingers over his back, winding her legs with his.

And even as she gripped his waist, Sam tried to erase his mind, to fill his thoughts with what would make Ashlyn happy.

Did he have anything that would fulfill her? Or would he always be dog-eared as "her first," the man who'd ushered her into the joys of sex?

Even as their skin heated, even as they slid the sheets off the bed corners, Sam knew that he had nothing to offer Ashlyn. Nothing but a sheltered heart and a willing body.

She deserved more than Sam Reno. More than the slow stretching heat of their bodies could provide.

Her nails scratched over his skin, her body tightening, flexing, a low moan signaling her release.

His world shot up to the moon, exploded with a shower of sparks then crashed around him with the sizzle of conscience.

He held Ashlyn, felt her clinging to him as their breathing evened out. He couldn't help caressing the nape of her neck, her hair, the slope of her cheek. The skin beneath his fingertips seemed as pink and warm as a long drink of fizzy champagne. His lips tingled, wanting more of her.

He bent down, brushing her mouth with his. The kiss was endless, languorous. On her lips he tasted everything from cherry soda on a hot summer's day to moon-clear water from a woodland stream.

He tasted the possibility of contentment, pure happiness. A lifetime of promise and fulfillment.

As he wrapped Ashlyn in his arms, feeling her body slicked against his, he wondered if he could take the chance of being hurt again.

* * *

They'd made love late into the night, the soft thuds of the completed record fading into the chirp of crickets outside his bedroom window.

Ashlyn stretched awake, loving the feel of Sam's sleeping body next to her. His arm felt heavy as it draped over her stomach, his breath soft with a lost innocence as he rested his mouth against her bare shoulder.

Last night had been perfect. She'd always hoped that the first man to make love with her would be The One—the man whose name was written in the stars next to her own.

She turned her head, watching him. Watching the man she loved, the man she needed to betray—even if it would be only for a short time.

His skin was dark against the white sheets, his bedroom walls as blank as his unspoken past.

She wanted to know everything about him now. Wanted to hear the memories that shaded his eyes. It was crazy, yes, but something inside her wanted to open that Pandora's box.

After all, wasn't she a part of him, even in some small way?

Something whispered inside of her, clawing at her heart. If she was so much a part of him, why hadn't she turned over the factory ledger? After all, if she took the evidence straight to her father, she'd be hurting herself as well as Sam. But she needed to hear her father admit his guilt out loud. Wasn't that the fair thing to do?

Sam's soft kiss urged her away from the thought. Her shoulder tingled against his mouth.

"Hey," he said.

The simple word seemed loaded with meaning. *Hey, what are you thinking about? Hey, I've made*

*love with you, but I'll never love you. Hey, you're
going to choose your family over mine.*

She rolled to her side, facing him, sketching a
finger over his lips. His hand fit perfectly at her
waist, and he used his thumb to rub against her
stomach.

"How awake are you?" she asked.

"I'm not talking in my sleep, if that's what you're
asking."

She could feel him smiling in the dark. "Sam,
remember Jo Ann Walters?"

He stifled a groan into his pillow. "Oh, no. Is this
the start of all those torturous past-relationship questions? I've already admitted my fascination with
Princess Leia."

His thumb intimately slipped into her belly button, giving Ashlyn a thrill that zipped straight down
to her curled toes.

"Yeah." She scooted closer, fingernails scratching down his chest, feeling the brush of hair rooted
among muscle.

He shifted under her touch. "Sure. I remember Jo
Ann Walters. We dated eons ago."

Ashlyn sat up in bed. "I want to show you something."

"Another man in the moon?"

She grabbed the comforter to wrap around her
body as she left the room.

"Ashlyn?" She could hear him sitting up in bed,
probably wondering what the devil she was up to.

She'd gone to her pile of clothes, the ones she'd
discarded before taking a bath and dressing in his
button-down and boxers. Sam's red ribbon was tied

around a bra strap, and she unwrapped it, fingering the faded, red silkiness.

When she returned to the bedroom, she opened the curtain slightly to beckon in the moonlight.

Sam reclined against the headboard, the sheet bunched around his waist, covering everything from there on down. His hair was mussed from the play of her fingers, and Ashlyn couldn't help feeling another zing of desire.

She climbed back onto the bed, biting her lip as she held out the ribbon to him.

He looked at it, at her, then back, evidently not making any connection between a piece of satin and her long-held fantasy of romance.

Of course he wouldn't know what this was all about. How could he understand a little girl underneath the football bleachers, watching him kiss the head cheerleader, thinking he was the most romantic thing since chocolate-covered candy?

Ashlyn smiled shyly. ''Once upon a time there was a little girl, Sam. She'd just been through the fright of her life, in a cave-in that taught her how unimportant she was. This girl just about worshiped Jo Ann Walters, her blond curls, the way she walked down the streets of Kane's Crossing like a princess. Everybody loved her, including her boyfriend.''

Sam leisurely crossed his arms over his chest. His muscles bulged, reminding Ashlyn of their protective strength, the feel of being secure and wanted.

He said, ''Aren't you overstating things? Jo Ann and I dated for maybe a month.''

''Well, back then I didn't know you were trying to break the world's record for most broken hearts.''

Was Sam Reno blushing? Ashlyn had always wondered at the depth of his vulnerable side.

She ran a finger over the ribbon, knowing that side had made love to her tonight. "It was after a game. Spencer High had won, of course, and everyone was celebrating. Jo Ann was waiting for you to come out of the locker room. When you did, you had flowers. Beautiful bunches of flowers."

Sam chuckled. "I couldn't afford more than a few, Ash, what with my measly job sweeping out the general store."

"Okay, so maybe I turned the whole thing into an overblown fantasy."

Maybe? Ashlyn cleared her throat, suddenly feeling foolish. Why had she even started this story?

"And?" Sam was still grinning.

Encouraged, she continued. "You gave Jo Ann the flowers, and you made her so happy. She dropped the ribbon—" she thrust it out at him again "—and didn't notice. I ran over to pick it up, and you saw me. You smiled."

Sam reached out for it, his face gone serious. "You kept it all these years?"

"I know. Weirdo," she said, trying to laugh. "I also kept a lobster shell that my dad had brought back from a fancy dinner one night, I guess in an effort to win me over after the cave. I'm a collector of memories."

"Damn." His voice seemed choked, and he steeled his jaw, a muscle jumping.

Ashlyn wondered what was going through his head. Did he think she was a strange pack rat, nothing more? Or—by some miracle—had he been touched by the ribbon?

Was he wondering why she had it with her to-night?

He opened his mouth, and she thought maybe he was going to ask. Just as quickly, he clamped his lips together.

Something he'd said earlier tonight slammed her thoughts. *No more confessions.*

He wouldn't want to hear why she'd kept the rib-bon; that she'd fallen for him the first night they'd met; that she'd dug it out of her memory book, need-ing more than anything to cling to a piece of hope and beauty.

All the same, she didn't even try to take the rib-bon back. He seemed too preoccupied with it, as if drawn to the past as willfully as she.

He swallowed, his Adam's apple bobbing, mak-ing her want to cover him with her body, pulling a sense of belonging from his warmth.

She said, "I didn't mean to make you sad."

Sam focused on her again, his eyes gone blurry from the tears gathering in her eyes.

She wanted to bite her tongue at his stunned gaze. Right now he was probably regretting making love with her, was probably telling himself that she'd taken his advances way too seriously.

A sob lingered, on the edge of bursting out, un-invited.

"Come here," he said, as if sensing her sadness.

He held out his hands, and she covered her mouth with a shaking fist, going over to him to press her cheek against his chest. Tears stung in her eyes as he wrapped his arms around her.

"Ash, if you only knew what kind of guy I am."

Her cheek burned against his skin, his heartbeat

punching at her eardrum. "You're the best of guys, Sam."

"Not if you asked my wife, Mary."

She held her breath, and his arms tightened around her.

When he stayed silent, Ashlyn chanced a question. "Wasn't she everything to you? The moon, the stars, the sun?"

He absently brushed his fingers back and forth on her arm. "At first, yeah. But I have to tell you, things weren't all that great. Especially the night she died."

His statement sideswiped her. Was she hearing him correctly? She thought Mary had been everything to him.

Ashlyn took his other hand and ran her lips over his knuckles. "Tell me, Sam," she murmured into his skin.

His sigh seemed to hold years of suffering. "We got married pretty quickly. My parents had just passed away, and I suppose I was lonely. I needed something besides police work, murders, drug deals in my life. And then came Mary, a schoolteacher, kind and loving. She seemed to be the type of wife I needed."

"So you married her?"

"I did, after knowing her only two months."

"Wow," she said, wishing she could think of something deeper to sustain him.

"Exactly."

He rubbed his mouth against her forehead, forming words against her skin.

"It was a good life at first, and we did love each other. But, at some point, the bottom dropped out of our relationship, and the thought of love seemed to hold us together more than the actual emotion itself. Dinners together grew quieter and quieter, until, eventually, we just had nothing to say to each other.

"In my misguided attempts to feel less pain in my life, I started talking about having children."

Here, Ashlyn felt her heart contract, fisted by jealousy.

He continued. "But Mary didn't want kids, not yet. Said she had too many running around the classroom each day and didn't have energy left for her own. I should've just let it go at that, but I didn't. That's what a thick head gets you. More trouble and heartache.

"A couple months down the road, after the meth lab debacle, after I'd quit the police force, Mary sat me down on a comfortable living room chair and announced that she was pregnant. Part of me was ecstatic, but the other part knew that she didn't want this child. And she told me that."

Ashlyn shook her head, causing Sam to frown and lean his head against the bedpost.

She said, "I can't understand that. Could you imagine if Tag's parents hadn't gone through with having him?"

"You're right." His arm settled around her waist as he paused, perhaps thinking about their mutual Little Brother.

After a moment he continued. "I made a fool of myself, begging her to keep the child, buying furniture, books, blankets for a nursery. But she threw it right back at me. 'Why would I want a cynical man to be this baby's father?'"

Sam paused, then cursed under his breath, his voice cracking. "I didn't know how to answer that. But, stubborn as I am, I tried to change her mind, to convince her that this baby would somehow mend our marriage. We argued. She ended up running out of the house and hopping into her car, screeching off into the night. The next time I saw her, it was when I was identifying her body at the crash scene."

His voice broke altogether, and he lowered his forehead to Ashlyn's. Something wet and filled with pain coated her skin. She wrapped her arms around him even tighter, hoping to hold on, to bring him back to her.

"I never did get to see our baby," he whispered.

"I'm so sorry, Sam." Ashlyn sat up, holding his face in her hands.

A red haze surrounded his hazel irises. "It's nothing for you to apologize about. I made my own mistakes, and I've been living with that guilt for too long, trying to make it better by living like a monk. For a while, I thought moving back to Kane's Crossing would help. I'd be around Nick's family, seeing that love is still possible."

He didn't say anything more. She wished she could show him that love was everywhere, especially in her.

What could she do to comfort him? To make life bright and full of wonder again?

As she pressed her lips to Sam's, she again wondered if her love would make him happy. She could shout her love, rumbling the walls of this house, bringing a smile to his face, if she thought it would help.

But Ashlyn knew it wouldn't. Even if he'd held

her in his arms, helping him to realize that he wasn't responsible for his wife's death, she wouldn't be able to lighten the darkness of his gaze.

All she wanted to do was to apologize to Sam, for his misfortunes, for the way she could make him feel less pain in them.

Yet, even in the dark of night, where shadows hid her intentions, she knew that, come tomorrow, she'd confront her father, even if it meant Sam would have to wait for his own opportunity.

She cuddled next to the man she loved, wondering if the emotion held any room for disloyalty.

In her heart of hearts, she knew it didn't.

Chapter Fourteen

The next morning Sam awoke to the twittering of springtime bird songs outside his window. He felt himself smile, reaching out to the space next to him in bed.

It was empty, cold.

He opened his eyes, finding a dent in the pillow where Ashlyn had slept. A red flower ribbon took her place, a reminder that last night hadn't been a dream at all.

He leaned on his elbow, grabbed the ribbon, fingering it as he had Ashlyn's short hair. Why hadn't she woken him up when she'd left?

Sam shook his head. Why even ask? He'd probably scared her off with his tales of woe—sob stories about Mary and their unborn child. No wonder Ashlyn had fled.

But she'd left the ribbon. And Sam knew that

Ashlyn placed a great deal of faith in symbols, in memories. She made a living making jewelry and sculptures—objects that meant much more than first met the eye.

Sam got out of bed, his muscles pleasantly aching. On the way to the shower, he couldn't help grinning as he rubbed the ribbon between his fingers.

Ashlyn had kept this for years. She'd obviously had some sort of young-girl crush on him—or the thought of him—and he'd had no idea. It was flattering, actually, to think that he held such an esteemed place in her sharp mind.

There'd been a moment last night when he'd wanted to ask why she had the ribbon with her. But he'd been afraid of her answer, afraid that she would say something as earth-shattering as "I love you."

He didn't want to hurt her with love. He didn't want to hurt himself, either.

As Sam turned on the shower water and tossed a towel onto the sink counter, he caught sight of a box of condoms, the contents scattered from haste.

With a start, he realized that they hadn't used condoms every time they'd made love last night. At one point he'd even woken her up with his kisses and caresses, and they'd gotten so carried away that neither of them had protected themselves.

His next thought stunned him. Ashlyn's babies. Kids with sparkling eyes and ready smiles.

His and Ashlyn's kids.

Dammit, you've been through this before. Don't do it again.

He wouldn't think about it now. He had a big day ahead of him. He and Gary Joanson were interviewing for additional deputies. He needed to contact Rachel Shane's newly hired private investigator. And he had to do more research about the factory to make sure that no more accidents hurt anyone in Kane's Crossing.

Once again he thought of Ashlyn in the cave, the suspicion that she was hiding something from him.

Sam stepped into the shower, hoping the hot water would wash his mind. But that didn't happen.

All he could think about was Ashlyn's softness, Ashlyn's smile. And, Lord help him, he held on to every thought, stowing them in his own mental book of good memories.

Two hours later, on the other side of Kane's Crossing, Ashlyn Spencer waited in her father's office in the mansion, her knuckles turning white as she fisted her hands.

When she'd arrived home minutes before the sun rose, she made sure no one knew she'd been out for the night, rumpling her bed, playing dumb when the maid asked how her night had fared.

She'd tried to push aside her guilt concerning the way she'd left Sam sound asleep in bed. She hadn't even left a note.

But she *had* left the ribbon and, to her, the object held more meaning than words. She only hoped Sam would understand.

The ribbon, in all its time-worn beauty, still held the colors of her love. And maybe, after this factory stuff had passed them by, she and Sam could forget everything else and be happy together.

As happy as they'd been last night, kissing, making love, sharing secrets.

Ashlyn was more than ready to begin erasing her family's mistakes. She'd already showered and called her father at the factory, telling his assistant that it was urgent business. That it had to do with the factory ledger.

As anticipated Horatio returned her call promptly.

Now, as Ashlyn sat in the brown-shaded room, she took a deep breath. She hadn't brought the ledger; there was no reason to. She had every detail memorized, charred into her brain, branding her with guilt.

She took a deep breath to quell the nerves that were even now nauseating her. Her gaze roamed her father's office: the jungle of potted plants, the over-fed leather chairs, the velvet curtains blocking sunlight. Even his antique French-walnut desk provided an intimidating plateau, housing everything from a gold-encrusted crystal pen holder to a gilt-framed picture of his two beribboned Maltese dogs staring innocently at the camera.

The door creaked open and, as the faint light increased, a shadow loomed larger and larger against the office walls.

Her father's voice split the air. "What mischief are you planning now, Ashlyn?"

She leaned back in the leather chair, attempting to pull off a corporate-like posture. Weeks ago, before she'd gotten to know Sam, she would've assumed a flippant demeanor. But those days were gone, swept into the past.

"Good morning, Father. I believe it would benefit us both if you'd look at this meeting in a different light. I'm here to discuss business. Very serious business."

His sigh of impatience grated at her nerves.

"Can this wait until dinner? My time is more valuable than this."

Anger flamed in her veins. "Everything seems to be more valuable than I am, Father. Come in and sit down, because I think you'll want to hear what your court-jester daughter has to say."

He paused, obviously taken aback. Then he stepped into the room, flicking on a light that suffused the walls with a brandy-tinged burn. With typical aplomb he sat in his mammoth chair, folding clasped hands under a rock-hard chin, spearing his gaze into her.

He said, "If you know about the ledger, I don't need to check my files to see that it's missing, to second-guess you. How dare you steal it from my belongings."

"And how dare *you* be so greedy." Ashlyn felt herself losing control, starting to tremble like a little girl in the face of her father's disapproval. She tilted her chin up. "How dare *you* destroy machinery in a cave, on the sly, so you wouldn't have to suffer the penalties of using inferior equipment and slouching off on the upkeep of it. How dare *you* blame Charlie Reno for killing those other men when all he was trying to do was save one from getting his hand mangled. How dare *you* keep using that same cheap, rotting machinery to squeeze an extra buck out of the business."

"Are you quite through?" asked her unflappable father.

"No, I'm not. I'm just warming up." She sat forward in her chair. "For years you've put those workers in danger, and you know it. When Nick

Cassidy purchased the factory and gave it to the poorer families of Kane's Crossing, they didn't realize what was going on. However, the new owners did hear the grinding gears. They shut down that factory and, when you bought it again, you made everyone believe you'd bought new machinery. But you've only changed the serial numbers, haven't you?''

She suppressed a shudder. ''It's just a matter of time before another accident happens, Father. How could you?''

Her father raised a cool brow. ''If I thought you had such a mind for business, I'd have put you in charge long ago.''

Ashlyn kept her calm, too full of rage to form words.

He got out of his chair, strolled over to the bar by the shuttered windows. As he poured himself a snifter of brandy from the bar—at nine-thirty in the morning, no less—his hand shook, causing the liquid to splash onto the teakwood.

A flash of hope flew through her. Horatio Spencer was nervous. Did that mean he had the capacity for guilt and, thus, the capacity to change?

She lowered her voice, sounding calmer, more open to his confession, if he cared to give it. ''Father, is money so important that you'll risk lives for it?''

He slammed his drink on the desk, shattering the glass, sending brown liquid over his Versace suit. ''We have no money, Ashlyn. Not after Nick Cassidy stole it. I've been borrowing from the Europe Spencers for over a year now.''

He stiffened his spine, probably thinking he'd said too much. "Where's that damned ledger?"

"We can discuss it later."

Horatio's dark glance held fury and maybe even a touch of regret. "I never thought I'd see the day when my own daughter betrayed me."

Wait. Couldn't he see that she wasn't betraying *him?* That she might've gone to Sam first? Maybe even *should've* gone to Sam first?

She opened her mouth to speak, but a frail, slurred voice interrupted her.

"Horatio, why are you yelling?"

Her mother stood in the doorway, a pale vision dressed in a tatted-lace nightgown, the white of the material casting an agonizing pallor over her skin. Her drug-misted blue eyes settled on Ashlyn.

"Dear, what have you done now?"

Ashlyn's throat choked up. She'd always held a dream that, one day, her family would talk to each other about more important things than dinner menus and society events. Could this be that day?

She got out of her chair and helped her mother to the settee, surprised at the strength in the woman's grip. "Sit down, Mother," she said.

Edwina Spencer followed her daughter's advice, facing her family with hands folded properly in her lap. "I could hear yelling down the hall, Horatio. What's so upsetting?"

Ashlyn placed her hands on her hips, sighing. "Let's stop this lying right now, Mom. Dad."

Her father's shoulders straightened at the informal address, but Ashlyn was beyond caring.

"I don't understand, Lynnie," said her mother.

"Stop it, Mom. You know what he's been doing

with the factory. I'll even bet you were standing outside the door the whole time we were talking."

Edwina's cheeks flushed, and Ashlyn knew she'd hit the nail on the head.

Her mother started crying. "I don't believe a word of it. Horatio?"

His lip curled, his tone commanding. "Don't worry about it. I handle the business. Don't make it your concern, Edwina."

She bowed her head, pulling her lips together.

Ashlyn saw the color red, blinding her gaze with memories. Bad ones. "Is this how it was with the cave-in? Is this how it was when one of you made the decision to risk my life for Chad's?"

Horatio stepped out from behind the desk. "Why you little ingrate."

Her mother sobbed. "I'm so sorry, Lynnie. We had to choose. It was the hardest thing I've ever had to do..."

Ashlyn wanted to crumble into a pile of shattered dreams. She whispered, "You made the decision, Mom? Why?"

"It doesn't seem fair, does it, Lynnie?" Her mom held out her hands, pleading. "He was the heir to the Spencer fortune. You were second born."

"And second place." Ashlyn sank down into the chair, unable to stand any longer. She'd always known the reason for being second best; she'd just needed to hear it. Just as she'd needed to go back to the cave to find evidence of the destroyed machinery. Just as she'd needed to hear her father admit to his guilt, as well.

"I know you can't forgive us," her mom continued, ''and I can't forgive myself. Neither can your father, if he ever had the gumption to admit it.''

''That doesn't change the choice,'' said Ashlyn.

Horatio was shaking his fist by his side. ''This is all in the past. It's useless to talk about. Ashlyn, you've had a damned good life here, not having any responsibility, running around town, embarrassing the family with your self-indulgent pranks. And now…''

''Now what, Dad?'' She dared him to say something about Sam.

His eyes held a suspiciously wet gleam. ''Now you've become the town whore, haven't you? Running around with Sam Reno, flaunting your disloyalty to this family. Are you proud of yourself, Ashlyn?''

She thought of Sam's strong arms, Sam's painful secrets that he'd trusted her with.

''Yes,'' she said. ''I am proud.''

She stood and walked out of the room, leaving behind people who didn't think she mattered. What killed her the most was that she knew with all her heart that she did matter to two individuals on this earth—Sam and Taggert.

And she'd just betrayed one of them.

Her father's voice stopped her cold. ''I want that ledger.''

''What good will it do you in jail?'' She turned her head, taking a calming breath. ''I love you, do you know that?''

Silence.

Anguish, tearing through her with the slow speed of thunder.

To fill the emptiness, to fill her conscience, she

whispered, "You need to pay for those factory deaths."

He didn't say a word. Not a damned word.

When she looked to her mother, she received the same response. Edwina simply looked past her, hiding, again, behind her painkillers, behind her excuses.

"You know—" Ashlyn's voice ended with the dry twist in her throat. When she'd swallowed it away, she continued. "All I ever wanted was your love."

And they stayed silent, telling Ashlyn everything she needed to know about how much she meant to them.

She couldn't believe it. She *was* nothing. Not even second place. As meaningless as one of many spots of darkness in a cave, as faceless and nameless.

But there was one optimistic, little-girl-crying-for-love flame left in her.

"Turn yourself in to the sheriff, Dad. If you cooperate…"

Both her parents killed her with a look.

She averted her own gaze. "Just so you know, I've already given the ledger to Sheriff Reno." There. Maybe that would convince them to repent.

Her parents glanced at each other. Her mother spoke first, her voice steadier than Ashlyn could have thought.

"You're a fool, Horatio. Settle this."

A sense of horror rushed into Ashlyn's soul, cold as fear's fingers, ripping out her insides, making her fall from Spencer grace completely.

She needed to get out of here, to warn Sam before her father could find him.

Sam was in the bakery, having gotten the bulk of his daily work done, laughing with Meg, when the newly hired dispatcher reached him with the message that he needed to call Ashlyn Spencer right away.

Meg wiggled her eyebrows. "What's that all about, Sam?"

He stifled a grin, hardly succeeding as memories of last night heated his body. He'd intended to call on her himself, but it looked as if she'd beaten him to it.

"Who knows what runs through the minds of you womenfolk," he said, hoping to high heaven he wasn't blushing like a kid. "She probably wants to do something with Tag tonight."

Meg shook her finger at him. "That's a convenient excuse. Now, you'd better get on the horn and call her before she unleashes her wrath on you, Sam."

His stubbornness almost didn't allow him to rise from his chair, but...what the hell. He didn't know if he could downplay his attraction to Ashlyn for much longer. It took too much energy.

Just as he was about to rise, the bells on the bakery door jangled, filling the post-breakfast emptiness of the room with some sound.

Meg's mouth fell open, causing Sam to look behind him.

Horatio Spencer scowled at him, eyes dark with disdain. "You have something that belongs to my family, Sheriff?"

For a moment Sam thought he was referring to Ashlyn, and he felt about sixteen, caught in a rumble seat with a cop's flashlight shining in his and his date's eyes.

Then reality hit. Business upset Horatio more than his daughter did.

"I don't know what you're referring to, Mr. Spencer." Sam turned back to his coffee and pie, aware of Spencer's taut body in back of him.

Horatio cleared his throat, and Sam took great pleasure in ignoring it. Hadn't the man learned by now that nobody in the Reno clan was—or had ever been—his puppet?

"I'd appreciate your cooperation, Sheriff. Please turn around."

Sam grinned at Meg, who then left the counter to go to the jukebox in the corner, choosing songs to relieve the tension no doubt.

A Big Bopper tune filled the air, hardly replacing the discomfort. Sam finally turned around.

Horatio lowered his voice, music covering the conversation from Meg. "Thank you. I want you to know, Mr. Reno, that I'm planning to get you fired."

Sam laughed. "And why is that?"

"I know you have important information about my factory, and it's obvious you haven't done a damned thing about it." He leaned in, speaking softly. "One way or the other."

Narrowing his eyes, Sam asked, "What the hell are you talking about?"

Horatio calmly took a seat next to him. "Let's not play this game. I know you have my factory ledger. And I know what its contents could do to me. I'm merely wondering why you haven't made an arrest yet.''

Sam's head swam. Had he lost his mind over Ashlyn to such an extent that he'd forgotten evidence? Did he have something in his possession that incriminated Spencer, and he just didn't know it? He needed to play his hand carefully.

''I move in my own time,'' he said.

''Hear me well, Reno.'' Horatio avoided his gaze, his jaw firm. ''If you want to get reelected, you'll do as I ask. You're already suspect because you've sat on this evidence. Understand?''

Sam's temper threatened to get the best of him. ''You're speaking in code here, Mr. Spencer. Speak in details. Concrete details.''

''Damn you, Reno. You're as hardheaded as your father.'' Horatio paused. ''An unfortunate incident, that. And I have to say I'm almost proud of Ashlyn for taking me to task over it. But, I'm a Darwinian by nature. Survival of the fittest, you know.''

Sam remained silent, hoping it would make him look as if he had more information than he did. He swigged his coffee, apparently unconcerned with Horatio's problem.

Horatio shook his head. ''That ledger she gave you is invaluable, but something tells me you'd be willing to put a sum on it. Name your price, Sheriff.''

Stark, blinding realization hit Sam like a sucker punch. Ashlyn had evidence—evidence she'd withheld.

Images, ghosts, screamed over him: the people who'd been killed in the factory accident, his father's disappointed gaze, his mother's outspread hands as she'd cried to heaven when her husband had died…and the children who'd been killed in the D.C. meth lab explosion, blood running down their cheeks like tears.

They were all pointing fingers in his direction. *You trusted the wrong person again, Sam,* they said. *Where do you get off taking responsibility for our lives when you can't even make sound choices?*

Ashlyn had lied to him, lied with her angel's smile, lied with her receptive body last night. He'd seen rainbows in her eyes, but now he knew that he'd been wrong about the colors—all he'd seen was a mirage, a reflection of how things used to be in Kane's Crossing, before all the death.

The truth about her honesty felt like a sword he'd fallen on by choice. Once, he'd had honor. And he thought he'd regained it last night, with her hand brushing down his face, with her ribbon throbbing like a heart in the moonlight.

He reached into his pocket, felt the ribbon next to her necklace. For a short time, Sam had been the guardian of both—her heart and her pain.

Now he felt closer to the pain, blinding as a car crash flaming up the night.

Sam stood just as the jukebox paused to change songs. He felt as if a spotlight was on him, emphasizing his mortification and agony.

Hell, he didn't care who saw that pain anymore.

Slowly he shed his badge, thinking of how much it'd started to shine in the past week. Thinking of how he could've thrown it in the sky to take its place with the other stars.

He set the meaningless piece of metal on Meg's counter.

Horatio chuckled. "What's this, Reno? A flash of conscience?"

Sam didn't deign to answer, instead reaching into his pocket for the ribbon. He felt its silkiness one more time, wishing Ashlyn hadn't turned out to be just like her father.

He set it on the counter beside the badge, both having taken on a lifeless, colorless sheen.

He watched the citizens of Kane's Crossing—the ones he'd let down with his misguided trust—walk past the window, smiling at each other, chatting away as if the world wasn't pressing down on their shoulders. He wanted to apologize for his ineptitude. Wanted to run away from these people yet again.

The door flew open, bells screaming for attention.

Ashlyn stood there, breathless, face flushed.

Their eyes met. Hers seemed to be brimming with confusion, concern. She started to speak, but stopped when her gaze fell upon the counter.

Her bottom lip trembled when she caught sight of the ribbon next to the badge.

She had to know exactly what he was thinking. That he'd been betrayed, and she wouldn't get another chance to explain why she'd made love with him last night, why she'd given her loyalty to the one man who could make Sam feel less than human.

Sam turned to Horatio. "Your dream has come true. I resign."

The older man's eyes seemed to blaze with glory, then burn out. Was this an empty victory for all of them?

Sam squared his shoulders, looking past Ashlyn as he approached her. She didn't move, frozen in place.

"I am so sorry, Sam," she said. "I need to explain."

Tears had wet her lashes, spiking them into sharp darts. Sam tried to calm his heart, tried to tell himself that her betrayal didn't matter.

But it was no good. He ached inside, burning with a fever that obliterated his soul.

Yet part of him wanted to stay, to give her another chance. But he'd given too many chances to too many people who didn't deserve it.

No more. No more pain.

"Talk to your father," said Sam. His voice sounded foreign, vulnerable. "He's the one who wants an explanation."

She looked at the floor, something like shame pinking her face. "Sam, I—"

"There's nothing left to say." And, without another glance, without another word, he walked out of her life.

He wondered if, among his many bad choices, this was the worst of them.

Chapter Fifteen

The night was thick with presummer songs, mournful and dirgelike.

Inside Sam's house, the rooms stood empty, save for the filled cardboard boxes.

As Sam surveyed them, he couldn't believe he was packing again. And, to think, he'd been just about unpacked this morning, after he'd woken up with a love hangover from Ashlyn.

But too much had happened between their last caress and their last words. Lord knew where Sam was going now; he just knew he needed to get out of Kane's Crossing.

Maybe he'd abscond to the mountains, living by himself in a cabin surrounded by sheltering trees. Somewhere he could be emotionless, without identity. But would the foliage obscure what Ashlyn had instilled in him?

Sam exhaled, walked over to the window. He pulled aside the ancient curtain, a remnant leftover from the old man before him. Maybe, like this house and its former resident, Sam had grown wizened before his time, settling into his dead zone as if it was a grave.

As he peered outside, he caught sight of the moon. Ashlyn had told him it was a man, with a clownlike face. Sam inspected the craters, the bluish glow of nothingness.

He wanted to believe there was nothing there, but he saw the eyes, the smile, the fat nose.

Would he ever stop seeing Ashlyn's bright opinion of the world around her?

Sam threw aside the curtain, shaking his head of Ashlyn's influence. But that wasn't the only thing beating him with guilt.

He'd have to talk with Nick and his family about his sudden decision to leave. And as if that wasn't bad enough, he'd have to say goodbye to Tag, too. The kid deserved at least some explanation about his absence.

Self-loathing burned in his gut. Would he be creating more of a problem for a kid who'd make any dad proud? Tag might end up hating him, hating the world because the people he cared about always left.

How was he going to explain this to the people he loved?

Sam grabbed an open box and began stuffing it with his belongings. Time passed as sweat slid down his temples, as he tried to avoid the sight of his couch with its images of Ashlyn tempting him, a wool blanket cuddled around her shoulders.

He hated himself for being wounded by Ashlyn's

loyalty to her family because, if truth be told, he would've given his own family a chance to explain themselves, too. He couldn't be angry with her decision, especially since he knew how much she needed love.

So why was *he* leaving? Wouldn't he wound her even more?

He'd been right about being hurt again. He didn't think he could stand another Mary, with their arguments, their disagreement about something as fundamental in a marriage as a child. Sam Reno wasn't made for relationships, and Ashlyn shouldn't suffer for it.

He wouldn't be able to stand it if he and Ashlyn traveled the same dead-end roads. Wouldn't be able to bear the accusation in her gaze, the disappointment of having a husband who'd run fresh out of love.

He picked up the gramophone, cradled it into a box to be stored in the basement for the next owner. He was leaving because Ashlyn had already hurt him, as he'd known she would. He shouldn't have ever opened himself to her, allowed her to see the emotional scars of his past.

Sam couldn't stand any more pain.

A purposeful knock sounded on the door, making him hesitate. He wondered if it was Deputy Joanson, who'd caught him in the sheriff's office, packing up.

Joanson had given him the ledger, since Ashlyn had presented it to the deputy earlier. Before leaving, Sam had read the ledger's contents, inwardly raging at the evidence. Feeling proud of the way his father had tried to save a life before losing his own.

However, it was Joanson's job to make the arrests now, without Sam.

And from what Sam had heard, it wouldn't be easy. Gossip said that Horatio and Edwina Spencer had already skipped town.

He walked to the door. "Yeah?"

His sister-in-law's voice filtered through the wood. "Would you please open up? I've got Tag with me."

Damn. Now what would he have to say to the kid?

He opened the door, finding Meg with her arm draped over the child's shoulder. Tag's eyes were hard, his jaw clamped shut. He thrust a card at him.

Sam tried not to appear too sheepish. "Kid, let me explain—"

"That's a card I made with Miss Spencer," he said.

Accepting it, Sam looked at Meg for help. But she was having none of it, with her lips drawn together, her hands on her hips. He would've guessed she was angry with him if he hadn't detected a glimmer of sadness in her eyes.

"So this is it?" she asked. "You're really leaving?"

Sam couldn't speak, just peered at the card, the front decorated by washes of finger-paint color. He turned to the inside, and Ashlyn's red ribbon tumbled to the ground.

Meg's voice floated over his pain, his hatred of himself. "You probably don't know that Ashlyn intended to give you the ledger all along. She just wanted to confront her father first, to hear the truth. Do yourself a favor, Sam. Don't blame her for that."

Sam tried to remain nonplussed as he bent to pick up the ribbon. "Is this your writing, Tag?" he asked, avoiding the bittersweet reminder of Ashlyn's love and what he thought had been a betrayal.

Meg answered. "The author is in your backyard, not wishing to insult you with her presence."

An ambush. Weeks ago he would've been affronted by the attack on his privacy, but now he was strangely touched. It was hard to be gruff when people cared about whether or not you left them.

He leaned over to switch on the porch light, the dim glow emphasizing the words.

The message was simple. *My heart is yours. Please don't leave us.*

His fingers pressed the ribbon, his chest tightening, making it hard for him to look at Tag. But he did, finding the boy squelching a smile, his arms stretched out for a hug.

Sam bent, scooping the kid into his arms, cupping his curly head against his shoulder.

"You staying, sir?" Tag mumbled into Sam's shirt.

Sam closed his eyes. "It's not that simple, son."

Taggert pulled back, watching him, eyes bright. "You called me 'son.'"

And Sam thought, maybe, it could be that simple.

But not as far as Ashlyn was concerned.

He started to say something to Meg, then realized she was no longer on the porch.

Tag squirmed, and Sam put him on his feet. "Sir, let's go fishing again. I like all that fresh air, you know."

"Tag…"

He trailed off when he saw Ashlyn, waiting by

the corner of the porch, looking as if the world had ended. Sam's heart crashed to a standstill at the sight of her.

"Come on, Tag," said Meg, walking to the circular driveway that held her car. "You okay, Ashlyn?"

Ashlyn glanced at Sam, biting her lip, then nodded. Meg loaded Tag in the car and left them standing in awkward silence.

She folded her hands behind her back, lowering her gaze. "I wanted to respect your feelings and refrain from charging up here to see you. Mostly because I haven't been doing a good job of considering your well-being lately."

Sam's insides were a mishmash of confusion. On one hand, he wanted to reach out to enfold her in his arms, in his life. On the other, he wanted to keep distance between them, decreasing the chances of feeling his own patented brand of pain.

He nodded. "I heard your parents are gone."

"Yeah." Her pause spoke volumes of agony. "I wouldn't be surprised if they were out of the country by now."

Sam couldn't imagine being stranded by his own parents. They'd loved him until the day they'd died.

"I'm sorry to hear that." He held open the door, tilting his head toward his family room. "Why don't you come in?"

She paused, probably wondering why he wasn't demanding explanations from her. Then she climbed the stairs to the porch, brushing by him as she entered his house.

Almonds and honey wafted on the air as she passed, filling his head with crazy ideas. Ideas that had always been there, waiting for Sam to embrace them.

She stopped cold at the sight of the packed boxes. "So you *are* leaving. Meg told me as much, but I couldn't bring myself to believe her."

"I think it's best that I go." He should have been convinced of the idea, after repeating it to himself all day. But the words rang false.

Her back was turned to him, but it was still obvious that she'd started to cry. Her shoulders, under the protection of a pink angora sweater, shook. She whispered, "I can't apologize enough times, Sam."

"You don't need to apologize anymore, Ash. What's done is done." He reached out to touch her hair, to comfort her, but stopped himself.

She never caught the gesture. He saw her raise a hand, wiping her face. "After I found that ledger, I debated for hours in the cave. I didn't want to come out because that meant I'd have to choose between you and my family. Obviously I made the wrong choice. I really needed to hear my dad admit his guilt to me before I told you."

"I should never have put you in that awful position."

She turned around, eyes wide. "How could you be so nice to me when I did the worst thing possible? I left the person I love in the dark."

His heart seemed to stop. She'd said it, confirmed his worst fears, brought him to the point where he'd have to confront all the tear-your-hair-out disappointments love brought.

But where was the discomfort? Where was the pain?

The disturbing swirl of a black hole that doubled

as his life stopped, snapping into sharp focus. Here was the woman who'd brought curiosity back into his imagination, the woman who'd made him picture giggling, gurgling babies.

Their babies.

Not long ago he'd told himself that he cared deeply about her, but it was more than that. Everything seemed so much clearer with her standing in his house, standing in a room in his heart, waiting for him to forgive her.

Ashlyn stepped past him, toward the door. "I can't believe my big mouth. I told myself I wouldn't tell you, I mean, it's bad enough you know about that cockamamie ribbon story, right? But I had to push you over the edge with my need to divulge everything."

"Stop beating yourself up, Ash." Was this him, Sam Reno, wanting to hear more? To feel more?

She slowly turned back around. "Should I?"

"I want you to stay. I want *me* to stay. I…"

He lost the words in the confusion of his thoughts. Was he truly in love with this woman? And could he tell her without the threat of his past wrapping around his throat to choke him?

Ashlyn sauntered toward him, her jaunty pink sweater adding a glow to her cheeks, a smile to her lips. "You were saying?"

What the hell was he saying? "I think I need some time here, sweetheart."

She stopped in front of him, chin to his collarbone, peering up through those thick lashes. Heat wavered between their bodies, a jungle of emotions he wanted to clear.

"You've got all the time you need, Sam." She

put her hand on his waist. "And while you're thinking, let me say this. I'm never going to let you down again, not like life did. I'm going to see to it that nothing ever comes between us again."

Sam waited for past disappointments to flap around him, to haunt him as they usually did. But they had left, chased out by his love for Ashlyn.

Yeah, love. It'd been there, in the folds of his soul, for a while now. It'd peeked out when Ashlyn had hidden in the cave, worrying him, making him think he'd never see her again. It'd burst into a reality when they'd made love, but Sam hadn't recognized the emotion at all.

He'd been too busy trying to avoid love.

Sam took her hand, put his other palm on her waist. Music drifted through his head, slow clarinets and white-satin vocals, throaty bass beats and lazy trombones. They danced to their own tentative rhythm, looking into each other's eyes.

Emotion filled his voice as he said, "The only thing I want coming between us is our children, when they sit on our laps or when we rock them to sleep at night."

The tear streaks seemed to fade from her skin, and her smile lit up that room in his heart.

"Children?" she asked.

He smiled, nodded. "And I think Tag would be a good start. After all, we've done a pretty decent job with him so far."

A bright tear danced down her cheek. "I'd love, more than anything, to be in a family with the both of you."

Sam felt like a groom, standing with Ashlyn as his bride, her hair veiled by the filmy white of optimism. Someday soon, he'd watch her sashay into his arms, dressed in silk, glowing, reflecting his love.

Ashlyn nuzzled up to his neck, sighing. "I'm going to do everything I can to make you happy, Sam."

As they swayed together, Sam tightened his grip on the ribbon. And on her.

He led her to his room but, this time, there was deliberation in lieu of urgency. There was no mad dash to the medicine cabinet for the condoms, no need for any sort of protection anymore.

This time, as he peeled the angora sweater off her body, they slowed their caresses, shed their clothing carelessly, without reserve.

He hadn't packed his sheets yet, and they made good use of them, fisting them off the bed, tangling them in their legs as they rolled on top of each other, rubbed against each other.

Ashlyn laughed as the material covered her face. Sam eased it away, looking down at the woman who'd brought the sun back to him.

"I love you," he whispered against her lips.

A burst of happiness and comfort stole through Ashlyn, making her feel as if Sam could protect her from anything. Even the hurt her parents had laid upon her.

"Me, too," she said, "although I thought I'd be about eighty-two years old before you admitted it."

He tossed the sheet corner back over her face and, as she laughed, kissed his way down her breasts, sliding his tongue over the middle of her stomach, down to her belly.

The breath caught in her chest as she felt his

breath warming her even lower. He loved her until she cried out with all the contentment in her soul, until she fairly imploded with heat and tumbled madness.

Afterward, as they lay, sated, with her head on his toned stomach, Sam guided her to his lips. They tasted each other again. He still reminded her of the woods, of all the special things hiding beneath the surface of brittle leaves. But now there was a change to him—a lightening of his soul brought out by a glimmer of new sunshine and summer-grass breezes.

As they pulled away from the kiss, Sam ran a finger over her chin, exploring her skin. "You'll always be the best choice I ever made, Ashlyn Spencer."

She bit her lip to keep from crying. How could he say that when she'd been second place all her life, first to Chad, then to Sam's wife...

She could feel her insides melting. "Are you sure?"

He slanted her a grin. "First place with me, sweetheart. Always first place with me."

Ashlyn thought she'd never heard more beautiful words in all her life.

Epilogue

Six months later

In the midst of their neatly decorated bedroom, Ashlyn Reno backed away from the full-length beveled mirror, her calf-length peach dress barely hiding the round of her stomach. An autumn leaf lazed its way past the window, reflected in the looking glass as she ran her hands over her tummy.

Sam stepped behind her, cupping the bottom curve of their child's domain. "You're beautiful. No matter what you're wearing, wedding-day dresses or gunnysacks, you outshine every woman in the world."

She met his gaze in the mirror, and their emotions locked, an eternity of love in that one look. Sam felt his throat get choked up, felt his world open up to the sun like a spring bud.

After a moment she smiled and asked, "Is Tag ready for Janey's wedding yet?"

"He's got his little suit pressed. Figuring out if he should wear a bow tie or your run-of-the-mill long tie."

"I vote for the first. He was wearing one when Janey first saw him at church just after she recovered from her breast cancer. She'll think he's so cute."

Sam kissed Ashlyn's cheek, rubbing against the softness, the endlessly fascinating scent of her. "Don't tell him that. He wants to come off macho."

"Like his dad." She turned to him, snuggling to just beneath his chin, fitting against him perfectly.

Sam's life flashed before his eyes: their wedding, flower petals floating happily around them even though Ashlyn's family was in Europe, avoiding criminal charges; Tag's adoption, capped off by a color-burst party with red-white-and-blue cake and balloons; Sam's welcome return to the Kane's Crossing sheriff's position; Ashlyn's pregnancy, her face glowing as she cuddled against him one evening to tell him the news.

She sighed, her breath warming his neck, sending shivers down his body. "Sometimes I still can't believe Emma Trainor invited me to the wedding," she said. "I half expected the invitation to come via a bullet from her shotgun."

Sam tilted her chin up with a finger. "She's forgiven the past, Ash. It's time you did, too."

She smiled, chasing away the shadows in her gaze. "I think I can do anything for you, Sheriff. How can I deny the moon and stars to the man who gave me a family again?"

As he reached down to circle his hands over her

belly, he chose to not ruin the moment by saying something. Her hands covered his, and no words were necessary.

Once again, he'd made the right choice. He'd chosen to trust again, to love as much as his heart would let him. He'd chosen to live with the vibrancy shining in all the colors of Ashlyn's eyes.

And, as Tag called him from down the hall, Sam realized that Ashlyn had been such an obvious choice all along.

He kissed his wife's forehead. ''We'll be there,'' he called to their son.

Then he wrapped her in his arms, encircling her for all the years to come.

*   *   *   *   *

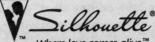

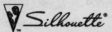
SINTBB

This Mother's Day Give Your Mom A Royal Treat

Win a fabulous one-week vacation in Puerto Rico for you and your mother at the luxurious Inter-Continental San Juan Resort & Casino. The prize includes round trip airfare for two, breakfast daily and a mother and daughter day of beauty at the beachfront hotel's spa.

INTER·CONTINENTAL
San Juan
RESORT & CASINO

Here's all you have to do:

Tell us in 100 words or less how your mother helped with the romance in your life. It may be a story about your engagement, wedding or those boyfriends when you were a teenager or any other romantic advice from your mother. The entry will be judged based on its originality, emotionally compelling nature and sincerity. See official rules on following page.

Send your entry to:
Mother's Day Contest

In Canada	In U.S.A.
P.O. Box 637	P.O. Box 9076
Fort Erie, Ontario	3010 Walden Ave.
L2A 5X3	Buffalo, NY
	14269-9076

Or enter online at www.eHarlequin.com

All entries must be postmarked by April 1, 2002. Winner will be announced May 1, 2002. Contest open to Canadian and U.S. residents who are 18 years of age and older. No purchase necessary to enter. Void where prohibited.

PRROY

If you enjoyed what you just read,
then we've got an offer you can't resist!

Take 2 bestselling love stories FREE!

Plus get a FREE surprise gift!

Clip this page and mail it to Silhouette Reader Service™

IN U.S.A.	**IN CANADA**
3010 Walden Ave.	P.O. Box 609
P.O. Box 1867	Fort Erie, Ontario
Buffalo, N.Y. 14240-1867	L2A 5X3

YES! Please send me 2 free Silhouette Special Edition® novels and my free surprise gift. After receiving them, if I don't wish to receive anymore, I can return the shipping statement marked cancel. If I don't cancel, I will receive 6 brand-new novels every month, before they're available in stores! In the U.S.A., bill me at the bargain price of $3.80 plus 25¢ shipping and handling per book and applicable sales tax, if any*. In Canada, bill me at the bargain price of $4.21 plus 25¢ shipping and handling per book and applicable taxes**. That's the complete price and a savings of at least 10% off the cover prices—what a great deal! I understand that accepting the 2 free books and gift places me under no obligation ever to buy any books. I can always return a shipment and cancel at any time. Even if I never buy another book from Silhouette, the 2 free books and gift are mine to keep forever.

235 SEN DFNN
335 SEN DFNP

Name	(PLEASE PRINT)	
Address	Apt.#	
City	State/Prov.	Zip/Postal Code

* Terms and prices subject to change without notice. Sales tax applicable in N.Y.
** Canadian residents will be charged applicable provincial taxes and GST.
  All orders subject to approval. Offer limited to one per household and not valid to
  current Silhouette Special Edition® subscribers.
  ® are registered trademarks of Harlequin Enterprises Limited.

SPED01   ©1998 Harlequin Enterprises Limited

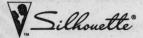

COMING NEXT MONTH

#1459 THE PRINCESS IS PREGNANT!—Laurie Paige
Crown and Glory
A shared drink—and a shared night of passion. That's what happened the night Princess Megan Penwyck met her family rival, bad boy Earl Jean-Paul Augustave. Then shy Megan learned she was pregnant, and the tabloids splashed the royal scoop on every front page....

#1460 THE GROOM'S STAND-IN—Gina Wilkins
Bodyguard Donovan Chance was supposed to escort his best friend's fiancée-to-be, Chloe Pennington—not fall in love with her! But when the two were abducted, they had to fight for survival...and fight their growing desire for each other. When they finally made it home safely, would Chloe choose a marriage of convenience...or true love with Donovan?

#1461 FORCE OF NATURE—Peggy Webb
The Westmoreland Diaries
A gorgeous man who had been raised by wolves? Photojournalist Hannah Westmoreland couldn't believe her eyes—or the primal urges that Hunter Wolfe stirred within her. When Hannah brought the lone wolf to civilization, she tamed him...then let him go. Would attraction between these opposites prove stronger than the call of the wild?

#1462 THE MAN IN CHARGE—Judith Lyons
Love 'em and leave 'em. Major Griffon Tyler had burned her before, and Juliana Bondevik didn't want to trust the rugged mercenary with her heart again. But then Juliana's sneaky father forced the two lovers to reunite by hiring Griffon to kidnap his daughter. Passions flared all over again, but this time Juliana was hiding a small secret—their baby!

#1463 DAKOTA BRIDE—Wendy Warren
Young widow Nettie Owens had just lost everything...so how could she possibly be interested in Chase Reynolds, the mysterious bachelor who'd just landed in town? Then Chase learned that he was a father, and he asked Nettie to marry him to provide a home for his child. Would a union for the baby's sake help these two wounded souls find true love again?

#1464 TROUBLE IN TOURMALINE—Jane Toombs
To forget his painful past...that's why lawyer David Severin escaped to his aunt's small Nevada town. Then psychologist Amy Simon showed up for a new job and decided to make David her new patient—without telling David! Would Amy's secret scheme help David face his inner demons...and give the doctor an unexpected taste of her own medicine?